The House of
The Fallen Angel

Rosemary Showell

Grosvenor House
Publishing Limited

This book is published by
Grosvenor House Publishing Ltd
Link House
140 The Broadway, Tolworth, Surrey, KT6 7HT.
www.grosvenorhousepublishing.co.uk

This book is a work of fiction. Any resemblance to
people or events, past or present, is purely coincidental.

A CIP record for this book
is available from the British Library

ISBN 978-1-83615-267-5

Prologue

It had been six months since we had left Heiligtum. Six months since the second gate had been closed forever. These dangerous doorways were the entrances to wormholes, tunnels connecting points in space and time, offering far quicker travel than through normal space. Our scientists hadn't known or even suspected that they had existed, but they had propelled my father, a brilliant young scientist called Luke, on a journey, not only across the universe but from one universe to another, one dimension to another, and one time period to another, until he became stranded on Earth.

These four wormholes have existed since the beginning of time and so Luke was not the only one to have used them – they had also been found by some of the evillest creatures in all of existence. If the remaining gates are not sealed forever, Earth will leave itself open to invasion by anything, from any galaxy, attacking any period in time.

There were now only two wormholes left, and thanks to the information found in the ebony box at Antique Treasures, I knew where to find them. One lay in or near Chateau Langedechu in France and the other in Castello Delcancello in Italy.

When Luke became trapped here in our world, for an unknown reason, he stopped ageing. Unable to return home and unable to stay in one place for any length of time, Luke moved from country to country, changing his name and moving on as soon as his prolonged youth was remarked upon. His advanced knowledge enabled him to amass a fortune. He built vast estates around the entrances to the wormholes, concealing them until he could find his way to control their power.

Eventually, he found a way to close them but that meant being trapped in our world forever. Through time, he met and fell in love with a young girl called Marianne, my mother. Marianne wanted a family but was unable to have a child, so Luke set about making one for her. In the process, he grew not one but four embryos. He implanted one in Marianne and then selected three other girls who were childless, alone, and who had no relatives who could ask questions and implanted them with one of the remaining test tube babies.

A brief time after my birth Marianne became ill and a devastated Luke couldn't save her. She was only twenty-four years old when she died. Luke, who was now enormously wealthy set, about creating an elaborate organisation to protect these four children, all girls, until they grew to adulthood. His plan was to leave them to inherit the estates that hid the wormholes. Lanshoud in Scotland, Heiligtum in Germany, Langedechu in France, and Delcancello in Italy. Luke set up his organisations in each of these countries. He put managers in place, loyal people who would raise and protect the four girls as they grew up. He even set up caretaker husbands for us and hired lawyers to manage our fortune. It had been so meticulously planned that it should have all gone well.

Luke had finally found a way to close the wormholes with what he called 'gates'. He manufactured 'keys' to for them too, but there was still a flaw in his plan: when he entered a wormhole to go back to his own world, he could not close the gate behind him.

Eventually, he went home anyway leaving Earth open to invasion by the alien beings who had been hunting him since he first passed through their world. A world we call Hell. He was now gone, and hopefully safe, in his own time and place, leaving me with the keys and the task of closing the gates. Somehow, I succeeded with the help of loyal friends who risked lives and souls to help me. Yes, the gates at Lanshoud and Heiligtum are now closed.

Chapter One

Rabbit at the Gard Du Nord

I had found my sister, Christina, at Heiligtum. Now I was about to search for Langedechu, another sister and another gate.

Having had their fill of the paranormal, Gill and Jack became completely focused on the raising of their son, whose incredible rapid growth from infant to child had been erased from everyone's memory, except mine. They both concentrated on their job at Lanshoud, which was to gather the treasures that were hidden there, by my father, and to take them to my shop called Antique Treasures in Byers Road in Glasgow. There Eli Laskov worked happily with Lily, his assistant, who had now graduated and worked full time in the shop, learning as much as she could about the antiques trade from the highly experienced Eli. Together they valued, listed and put up items for sale in the shop and on the newly updated Antique Treasures website. The money from these sales then went towards the upkeep of Lanshoud.

One of the managers in Katie's two gift shops was pregnant and she was taking extended maternity leave. Katie had not yet filled the temporary post, so she was managing that shop herself. Katie knew that I would eventually go to search for the third gate, and she was determined to go with me. I had no idea just how determined she was until I learned she had closed one of her shops until further notice. Knowing Katie as well as I did, there was no point in arguing with her; she had a steadfast sense of loyalty to her friends.

There was no way she was going to allow me to travel alone again, especially after that last fateful trip to Potsdam. Together, we travelled to London, stayed overnight at a hotel, and then took the Eurostar from St Pancras to the Gare Du Nord in Paris.

Katie truly believed I was gullible. She believed I was capable of being taken in by anyone who had, what she called, 'a sob story'. The problem is that, even when I am doing the right thing, Katie makes me doubt myself. If there is the slightest seed of doubt growing in my mind, Katie's whisperings in my ear can grow that seed of doubt into a forest. I have worked hard at portraying myself as a confident, smart businesswoman when I travel, yet Katie always manages to bring me back down to earth.

She remarked, "You look tired. You should close your eyes and take a nap." Even though she knows that, unlike her, I can never sleep on a train or a plane, she asked, "Did you not sleep well last night?"

"No, I didn't. I never sleep well the night before travelling anywhere, and I never have a good night's sleep anywhere but in my own bed." I replied – although Katie knew that too. "I am tired, Katie." I mused. "Maybe too tired for the things I plan to do when we arrive in Paris."

Katie shook her head. "Well, I did tell you that would happen. We should have taken a later train." She then surprised me by saying, "James called me last night to wish us a safe journey. When did he call you?"

I sighed because I knew what was coming. "He didn't call me. He sent me a text."

She sat up. "That's strange. Even though you devastated him by refusing his marriage proposal, I thought you might still be friends."

"We are," I said. "James sent me a text. I told you about it. It was about this friend or contact who is meeting us at the station, Peter Hopkins. He is the private investigator I told you about him."

Katie was quiet for a moment, then said, "Yes, well, just so as you know. I don't like the sound of him. English, unmarried, no family, living for years, alone in Paris. I mean, really, the city of romance? That's just weird." Then she said thoughtfully, "Maybe it's his looks that are the problem. James said to think rabbit when you're looking for him'. I bet he will have floppy ears and buck teeth… That could be a genetic link to his name, you know, the family being called Hopkins! I bet he had a tough time at school. It's a pity he's not good looking. I could do with hanging out with some, eye candy."

"Oh, for God's sake, Katie, what difference does his looks make? He is a private detective for hire and believe me, these private detectives are expensive."

"What! You are having to pay for his services? Some friend!"

"I insisted on paying. It's how the man makes his living, and it means I have someone I can trust, someone who knows the area, someone I can call for advice if we run into problems."

"You could have trusted James. You know you only have to snap your fingers and James Cameron would have been on this train with us! I am telling you now, I insisted on coming with you because I have a bad feeling about this, not just about the man Hopkins but about the chateau, not that you ever listen to me, even though you know I am always right about these things."

Unfortunately, that was true and so, with the seed of doubt now watered and growing fast, there was little chance of me taking a nap. However, while I gazed out of the window and worried, my psychological gardener closed her eyes and went to sleep and did not wake up until we reached the Gare du Nord.

I hadn't slept the previous night. Both Lanshoud and Heiligtum had been a nightmare, a brush with Evil incarnate, but I was rescued each time by beings of light. I had been stronger then because of the people around me: James, Jack and Gill. Here there was only Katie – Dear, sweet, dependable Katie – who drove me crazy at times but was as loyal as a guard dog.

I felt anxious about what I would find when I reached the chateau. I knew what Elise Du Sante would look like; after all, she would look like me and Christina – being the same age and having the same background story. She would be rich, brought up by surrogate parents and with a caretaker husband, like Paul Cameron and Frank Summers. Would she know the story of our father? Would she be wealthy, with a fortune having been left to her? Would she know she had three sisters? More importantly, would she know about the gates?

I hadn't seen James nor spoken to him since we had left Heiligtum. The WhatsApp text was the first communication from him since we had returned to Glasgow. It had been short and to the point. It read: *"Hi, hope you are well. As you will shortly embark on another search for your remaining siblings, and it's France you have chosen to search for the third gate, I enclose the contact details of a friend living in Paris. He is a well-respected private investigator, honest and trustworthy, who will help you in any way he can. His name is Peter Hopkins. He has lived in Paris for the last 15yrs. I have enclosed his address and telephone number. He is expecting you to call. The only information I have given him, is that you are searching for a long-lost sister. I have great respect for Peter – he is a clever man – however, he is a little eccentric, but please don't let that put you off. Travel safely, James."*

Later he sent another text message: *"Peter Hopkins has offered to meet you at the Gare Du Nord railway station. He will take you to your hotel. Watch out for him. He will be looking for you."*

I replied: *"How will I recognise him?"*

James: *"Think rabbit and you won't miss him."*

Me: *"Think rabbit?"*

James: "Exactly. Trust me – you won't miss him: there is only one exit from the platform onto the concourse. I sent your mobile number and a photo of you and Katie to Peter, so he will be watching out for you. He is over six feet tall and stands out in a crowd. He wears a tweed deerstalker hat, come hail, rain, or shine. Take care, James."

The train pulled into the Gare du Nord at 3.15 pm. We struggled to get off. The train had been full, and now the platform was heaving with people and luggage. Katie glanced around with horror. "How are we ever going to find Peter Hopkins in this crowd? James said there are 700,000 people arriving here daily. He didn't say they all arrive at the same time!"

She wasn't exaggerating.

"Watch your bag Katie, Gill warned me that this place has a reputation of pickpockets."

"Your phone just beeped," she said.

I hadn't heard it, and I struggled to find my mobile at the bottom of my bag. "It's a text from James. It says: 'Wait until the platform gets quieter. Turn your back to the platform where the trains lie. Look forward and up. There is a café on the mezzanine level. Peter will be sitting at a table waiting for you... PS remember to "think rabbit" and you will recognise him'."

The café was easy to find, but it was busy with every table taken. We stood there looking around, but there was no sign of anyone resembling the description of Peter Hopkins that James had given us.

"What now? Do we wait?" Katie asked, adding that she had to go to the loo. "Ok, go, I will order a pot of tea."

"Oh yes, and get me one of those," she said, pointing to the delicious pastries that you only ever see in French cafés.

Katie had just disappeared down a flight of stairs inside the café when a waiter appeared. He apologised profusely that we had to wait and escorted me to a recently cleared table.

Katie and I sat in that café for almost an hour and there was no sign of Hopkins. Tired and fed up, I said, "C'mon, let's go. He's not coming, is he? Or maybe we are in the wrong place, though I don't see how – there's no other café here. I think we should just leave. We might bump into him on the way out."

"Call him: James gave you his number," Katie said.

"No, I would rather not."

"Oh, for goodness' sake. Give me your phone. I'll call him," she said.

"No. I'll do it myself, when we are outside. Let's go."

As we paid the bill, we heard a commotion down by the trains. That was followed by an announcement in French over the loudspeaker and suddenly people were leaving their tables, scraping back their chairs as they headed for the door. Then the announcement came in English. There had been an incident and everyone had to make their way to the exits immediately.

"Katie, look! Over there."

From outside the café, we looked down on the tableau beneath. A body lay on the ground, with paramedics attending. I couldn't see if it was a man or a woman. There were police standing guard and people rushing towards the exits, some abandoning their luggage. There were armed police officers everywhere. One of them moved and we could see what looked like a man's feet.

"Oh my God, Katie! I think that might be Peter Hopkins."

"What? Why do you think it's him? Just because he's late?" she asked

"No because there on the ground between those two policemen, it looks like a deerstalker hat." I had a sudden horrible feeling of dread.

Pushed from behind by the exiting diners, we carried on downstairs and managed to get through the crowd, most of whom were rushing towards the exits. The police had formed a circle around the figure on the ground. There they were ushering and forcing the crowds away. As we passed the kneeling figures, one of the paramedics stood up, and for a second, I could just see a man lying in a pool of blood. He had a protruding jaw, and in his gaping mouth, buck teeth were visible. The deerstalker was lying on the ground beside him.

When Katie walked forward for a better look, one of the police officers grabbed her by the arm and actually dragged her away, speaking angrily in French. He pushed her forward.

Flustered, Katie said, "That's him, isn't it?"

I nodded. "I think so. Poor guy. I wondered what happened." Then I asked her, "Did you see anything else?"

"Yeah, he has been shot in the head, execution style." She said that as though she were some sort of expert. Before she could say any more, I was pushed forward and we were almost separated.

Katie caught up. "I think we should go back and tell them he was there to meet us; we can find out what happened.'

I said, "No." Even if that was a good idea, which it wasn't, we were still being pushed along by the crowd and there was no way back. "We don't even know this man," I said. "I don't want to get involved. They will probably be looking for us sooner or later anyway. Our photos and texts will be on his mobile."

"I saw it – the mobile; it was lying on the ground. It was smashed to smithereens," she said.

"Makes no difference. The police will get the information out of it anyway. I've watched enough detective programmes to know the police have that sort of technology."

At this point an argument broke; a fiery Italian lady was shouting abuse at one of the station workers, who had picked up her bag. He was giving as good as he got, though. All hell broke loose when her husband joined in, and it was obvious the couple didn't speak French, and the workers didn't speak Italian. That altercation stopped some of the crowd and gave us a chance to reach the exit.

There was a queue for taxis outside the station that stretched round the block.

There was also a melee of anxious people trying to flag one down.

"Oh, great, what do we do now?" I asked, not expecting an answer.

"Phone James. Tell him what has happened," Katie said.

"No, I'll call him later. That man might not be Peter Hopkins."

"You're right," she said dripping sarcasm. "Maybe it's a brother with the same unfortunate rabbit genes and who equally likes to wear a deerstalker hat. Don't be ridiculous, phone James."

"I will, when we get to the hotel."

Katie noticed that, directly across the road, there was a car hire garage. "Over there, look: we can hire a car."

"What use is that? Can you do left-hand drive? Because I can't!" I said.

"If we're lucky," she said, "you're about to find out."

The girl in the car hire spoke perfect English and expressed her horror at the incident in the station.

"News travels fast," Katie said, under her breath.

The girl was sympathetic, but she had no cars left for hire. I asked about the metro; she said that it would mean two changes and it would be difficult; it was always crowded at this time of day and would be worse now with the crowds evacuating the station. She said it would be better to start walking along Boulevard Haussmann and maybe flag down a taxi along the way.

I asked her how long it would take to walk to the hotel. She shrugged, "About an hour or an hour and a half." My heart sank. We did have trolley cases, but they still carried bags and jackets and other bits and pieces; it would be a pain to walk any real distance.

The girl went to answer the telephone. Katie grinned. "Got it. Bribe them."

"Bribe who?"

"Over there, look." She pointed. "Where? What am I looking for?"

"Those men standing about, or leaning on cars, doing nothing. I bet you they are salesmen, and they will all have their own cars."

She was right. Half an hour later, we were dropped off at our hotel. The salesmen knew we had no choice and so it was the most expensive short ride I have ever taken.

As soon as we checked in, I called James, but there was no reply. Katie kept trying. We left messages asking him to call back. There was no response.

The hotel was lovely, and the twin room was luxuriously furnished. I had booked it for a week to give us time to find our way to the Chateau Langedechu, though Eli told us it was only an hour away from Paris.

We decided to get some fresh air after dinner. I thought it might help me to sleep because the horror I witnessed at the station, seeing James's friend lying in his own blood, was hanging over me and I knew I would have trouble sleeping. Some fresh air would help.

We went for along the Canal St Martin. It was a beautiful Parisian evening. The atmosphere was lively with restaurants and café's open and busy. Teenagers lined the banks of the canal, picnicking in the evening sun, their music and laughter filling the air; any other time I would have loved it but not now.

I awoke early the next morning. Katie was still sleeping like a log. I made myself a cup of tea from the complimentary tray provided by the hotel. I checked my mobile; there was still no word from James. It was only around 6.15am. I couldn't call him as it was too early – it would only be 5.15am at home. I sent another text, asking him to call and almost jumped out my skin when the phone rang immediately showing James's number. I answered it, ready to apologise for disturbing him so early.

"Open the door," he said, his voice so low I was struggling to hear.

"What?" I asked, confused.

"I'm in the hotel, outside your door. Open it, quickly," he said, again in a whisper.

I ran to the door, unlocked it. He stepped in, quickly closing it behind him. "Wake Katie, get dressed, gather all your things, don't leave anything behind, we have to leave now."

"What? Why?" I asked, bewildered.

"I will be waiting in the car park in a blue Citroen. Move now, don't bother to check out and be as quiet as possible. Take the lift straight down to the basement carpark, avoiding the reception."

I went to speak. He said, "No time for questions. Erica, trust me; I am serious, you're in danger. I will explain in the car."

I nodded.

He whispered, "Hurry, wake her." He left, closing the door quietly behind him.

Katie, who always slept soundly, hadn't even stirred. My heart was thudding in my chest. I shook her awake and put my hand gently over her mouth before putting my finger to her lips. She woke with eyes like saucers. "Listen," I whispered, "something is wrong. James is here. He's down in the hotel car park. He said we're in danger. Get up and get dressed; we have to leave now."

She just stared at me in reply.

"Just do it, Katie."

She almost fell out of bed, pulling on her jeans. We just wore the clothes we wore the night before and, but it still took us only ten minutes to leave the room because we hadn't unpacked.

We found James easily; the Citroen was the only blue car in the car park. James opened the boot, put our luggage in and told us to get in the car.

"Give me your mobile," he said. "They are tracking you."

"Who are?"

"I'll explain later."

I gave him my phone. He took out the SIM card, cracked it and dropped it down a drain.

He drove up the ramp and, minutes later, we were in the street and heading out of Paris. I was sitting in the front seat. He asked us to keep an eye out for any car that looked as though it might be following us.

I blurted out, "James, I think Peter Hopkins is dead."

"Yes," he said sharply, "I know. We will talk about it later. Concentrate on looking out for any car that might be following us."

He was upset about his friend because he didn't speak again until we were well outside of the city. I had so many questions to ask, but he was tense and speeding, so I didn't want to distract him. After about an hour, he pulled off the motorway onto a side road. We drove through a sleepy little village, with its café's already open and with mostly elderly men sitting outside drinking coffee and smoking.

James turned off the road onto a dirt track and I saw the sign: 'Berny Rivière'. The track led into the countryside. It wasn't too long before, to my surprise, he drove into a caravan park. It was only 8am and there were already people queuing at the camp shop.

James pulled over beside the site office. He got out, saying, "Stay in the car."

Katie watched him disappear then asked, "What is going on? He didn't look in the least put out when you told him his friend was dead. You know James can be quite cold sometimes." I didn't answer; I was thinking the same thing. Then she snapped, "What the hell are we doing in a caravan park?"

"I know as much as you do," I said. "Maybe he's renting a caravan for us. This area is Picardy. L'Ange Dechu is near here.

There may not be any hotels nearby. As to James being 'cold', I think he's really upset about Peter."

"Maybe you're right and he won't want to burst into tears in front of us, but that doesn't explain why he drove out of Paris like a bat out of hell. Furthermore, why is he even here in France in the first place? Did he even suggest he wanted to come to L'Ange Dechu with you?"

"No. I don't know why he's here. It's James, Katie. We just have to trust him."

"I suppose," she grunted.

Five minutes later, James came out with a set of keys. He started the engine and drove at a snail's pace through the camp, stopping by some large static caravans, with gardens and hedges surrounding them. "Look for number twenty-one," he said, crawling the car forward. "We are staying here tonight," he said and, under his breath, he added, "and maybe for a few nights. I think this is the last place they would expect to find you."

"Hold on a minute... They? Who are 'they'?"

"Right now," he said "THEY could be anyone who has just walked past. We will stay here, out of sight."

"I think not. I have a luxury hotel booked for a week."

"No, you can't stay there," he said.

"I held up my hand. "James, stop – enough is enough. You are scaring the hell out of us. Who are THEY? Why are we here in a caravan park? And, for that matter, why are you even in France?"

Ignoring me, he said, "Number twenty-one. This is us."

He pulled into the caravan bay and parked behind the bushes, concealing the car from the road. He insisted on lifting our luggage into the caravan and then said, "I am going to get food from the camp shop. I will explain it all when I get back. Stay inside and lock the door."

With nothing else to do until he came back, I looked around. The caravan was spacious, with three bedrooms, a kitchen with a comfortable seating area and a small electric fire and TV.

There was also a toilet and a shower room and, outside, there was a deck with a barbecue. Katie collapsed on the sofa. "This would be great if we didn't have this drama that James is weaving around us. It's blooming weird." She grabbed handfuls of her black curls and groaned. "I am shattered, having been dragged out of bed at an ungodly hour and having the wits scared out of me. Do you know *anything*?"

"You know I don't, and you actually slept for ten hours, so I don't know how you can be tired."

She groaned again and stretched out, putting a pillow over her face before actually falling asleep, as only Katie can.

After about half an hour, James came back. He knocked and said, "It's me, open up." Katie emerged from under the cushion. "Oh, he's back? Let him in. I have more than a few questions to ask him, like how did he get here so quickly? And why does he not seem devastated by the probability his friend has just been shot dead?"

I opened the door, and James had clearly heard what she had said. He put the bag of groceries down and studied her. "I am not devastated, Katie, because I shot him. I killed Peter Hopkins."

Chapter Two

The Chateau Langedechu

"It was you who killed him!" I was stunned. Katie sat bolt upright, eyes like saucers and speechless for once in her life.

"You shot him! You killed your friend. Why?" I asked.

James didn't even turn around. "The fact is that it was him or you. He was not my friend."

"I don't understand," I said, watching him empty the bag of food onto the work surface.

Not looking at me, he said, "I didn't send those text messages. I did call Katie the night before you left, but I didn't text you."

"Yes, you did; those texts are still on my phone."

He turned and looked me straight in the eye. "It wasn't me you were communicating with. The first I knew about him meeting you was when Katie called me."

"You called him? When was that and why didn't you tell me? I asked her. She went all coy. "In the café, when I went to the loo."

I shook my head in disbelief. "You never said a word."

She shrugged. "I did tell you on the train that I didn't like the sound of Peter Hopkins but, if I had told you I was phoning James, you would have stopped me. Don't say that's not true."

"Probably, but why did you call him?"

She said, "My intuition, which as you know is incredibly accurate, was telling me there was something not right about this Peter Hopkins."

James sat down. "When Katie described him as the rabbit man. I knew who he was, and why he was there. He would have been meeting you for only one reason and that was to kill you. The man who called himself Peter Hopkins was Gunther Schulz, one of the Die Bruder gang. He was Dietrich Oppenheim's hit man. You are the only reason he was there, in the Gare Du Nord."

I sat down, my legs were turning to jelly. "Die Brueder, the brothers of the Fourth Reich, here in Paris! I thought we had heard the last of them."

James said, "Hopefully, you have now. All of Oppenheim's gang were jailed after Heiligtum, but Gunther Schulz was never caught. There are known to be a few of these cells scattered across Europe. Schultz may have come here and hooked up with one of them and, of course, after Heiligtum he had a score to settle with you.

My head was spinning. "So, they know about Langedechu? And the gate?"

"No, I doubt it. I suspect he just hacked into your mobile and found you were travelling to Paris. I have contacts in the French authorities who were tracking the Paris cell. They have assured me that, on this, Shultz was working alone. Still, it was better to be safe than sorry. That was the reason for our dramatic exit from your hotel. Even if you were of interest to the Paris cell, and unknown to the authorities, there may have been someone with Schulz in the station, they would still have lost your trail back in Paris. We are safe enough here."

I said, "But if they tracked us to Paris, then they can track us here."

"No. Remember that I destroyed your SIM cards in the car park at the hotel? Give me your mobiles and I will put these in." He took two SIM cards from the envelope.

James had been in Paris for nearly two weeks. Katie asked him why. "Business," he replied, in a tone that suggested it was none of hers. "I have also been to Langedechu," he said, watching me carefully. I knew James well enough to know he was not about to give me good news. He was speaking slowly, choosing his words carefully. "The chateau is empty and has been for a few years. I spoke to the local police, the gendarmerie. Do you remember the train crash in Paris about three years ago? The train that left the rails on a bridge and fell into the river. It was all over the news at the time..."

My heart sank.

"I remember that" Katie said. "Almost all the passengers and crew were killed. She reached out and squeezed my hand guessing, as I did, what he was going to say. I felt a knot growing in my stomach.

James said, "I made enquiries. I am truly sorry Erica, but I am afraid Elise, and her husband Anton Bernard were on that train. Anton's body was recovered but Elise's was never found."

She was dead, my sister, Elise. I would never know her. I had imagined what she would look like, wondering whether she would have been more like me or Christina. I had been excited at the thought of meeting her. I had practiced what I would say. Looking forward to her surprise. Telling her my story and telling her about Christina, and our father, Luke. Listening to her story. Sharing secrets with her. But she was gone, and I would never know her. I felt overwhelmed by a deep sense of loss. Strange, I suppose, when I didn't even know of her existence until two years ago, when Eli Laskov drew the paper and keys from the ebony box with the names of the houses and the four babies.

I sat there in silence, deeply disappointed, trying to take in what he had just told me. Then I asked, "Are you definitely sure they were on that train?"

"Yes. I have contacts in the DGIS, The French equivalent of MI5 – it's the department of counter espionage and counter terrorism. They monitor and deal with any threats on French territory. They are very familiar with Die Brueder, and Gunter Schultz and they are still investigating a possible connection between the train crash and the Die Bruder gang."

James drove us to the Chateau after breakfast. It took us less than an hour to get there. I don't know what I expected but the scene in front of us was so beautiful it took my breath away. Langedechu was a fairytale, lost in time. It reminded me of a scene from the movie Beauty and the Beast.

The vast gardens that surrounded the chateau were neglected and overgrown and it looked as though Mother Nature had waged war on the building after the occupants had left. Her army of trees and plants had almost succeeded in hiding the chateau completely from the rest of the world. Overgrown shrubs with thick vine-like branches had wound their way through the massive wrought iron gates. Gates that were chained and padlocked.

James pointed to a gap in the hedge. "I got in this way," he said, holding out a hand to help me through. Katie followed, complaining she had caught her jeans on a bush and ripped a hole in the denim fabric.

Katie was not happy. "Why is it things are never straightforward in your world?" she asked me.

"You know why," I said. "Anyway, you didn't have to come."

The stone path to the front steps was scattered with weeds. Vines grew up the walls and through broken windows. With no one to prune the trees and shrubs, they had spread wildly, creating a barrier around the chateau, shutting out the rest of the world.

James led the way, and we followed him up the stone stairs to the ornate front doors made of dark wood and studded with metal fleur-de-lys. He turned the ring on one door, and it creaked open onto equally unlocked inner doors. Inside the hall was a circular marble floor with the fleur-de-lys in the centre and six doors surrounding a staircase. The doors all lay ajar, giving us a view of the lavish décor and expensive furnishings.

We spent the next hour exploring. It looked as though no one had lived there for years.

"This is the dining room," James said, stepping into a beautiful room decorated in red and gold. There was a large table in the centre with chairs for eighteen people. Dust sheets covered the furniture. Ornaments and clocks had been removed from the shelves and placed on the table. Paintings were stacked against the wall, some were portraits, and some were views of Langedechu.

James pulled forward the largest one. "I think this is where the house got its name." The picture depicted a dark angel on the ground, its face contorted in fear. Standing over it, bathed in white light, holding a spear ready to strike, was another angel. He said, "There is a similar statue in the grounds. Hence Langedechu, the House of the Fallen Angel.

Under the stairs a little passageway led to the kitchen. An old fire hearth had been set with paper, wood and coal, ready to light. I opened one of the cupboard doors and found a vast amount of blue and white dinner service, cutlery, utensils and serving dishes. I picked up a large serving plate. The white porcelain was intricately decorated with ladies in large gowns and hats with huge feathers. The gentlemen, equally dressed in 17th century finery, posed in long coats, breeches and plumed hats. The detail on their buckled shoes was amazing.

A door from the kitchen led to a larder. The shelves were stocked with tins and jars still filled with spices, salt and sugar. I opened the sugar jar, but it was so old that it had turned into a solid block. Katie picked up a tin, she checked the expiry date. She went on checking tins of soup, meat, and vegetables.

"These are all good to eat, and look there…" She pointed to a shelf at the top. She took down a bag of sugar, still sealed and soft, and reached up again to lift down and open a tin of chocolate biscuits. "Do you think there is someone still living here? Squatters maybe? There is no way some of this food is three years old."

"You may be right," James said. "But they weren't here any time recent." He had picked up a pot sitting on the stove, lifting the lid saying, "Look." I wished I hadn't: it was full of a disgusting foul-smelling mould.

Back in the hall, period wallpaper, depicting riders on horseback chasing deer, hung peeling from the walls. Red velvet curtains hung from brass rails on the huge windows on either side of the front door. I followed James into what looked like a study. It had walls of bookcases, which were mostly empty, and a writing desk.

I said, "It doesn't look as though they had intended to return after that train journey. I mean, look at this." I showed him a large cardboard box filled with little China ornaments, each carefully wrapped in tissue paper and bubble wrap. "And look here: boxes and boxes, packed with books.

James took a penknife from his pocket and opened a larger sealed packing case. He lifted out a large book, which was blue leather bound and embossed with gold. He opened the pages and read, "This is a first edition of Bleak House. It must be worth a fortune." He lifted more books. They were all rare or first editions. He said, "It looks as though these things were being packed for sale just before they took that train journey.

Katie was standing at a stunningly carved wooden desk. "Look at these legs," she said. "They are carved into trees with the branches supporting the top. She picked a cloth from the floor and wiped the dust from it. The highly polished surface, with different hues of pale and blonde wood, gleamed in the sunlight pouring in from the window behind it. It was so highly polished it looked like glass.

There were little drawers on the top, at the back, and curved around the sides of the desk. Katie was opening and closing them, calling out their contents, paper clips and tacks, elastic bands, and pens. She pulled on one that seemed to be stuck and exclaimed, "Oh no!" when the front of the drawer came away in her hand. She tried to fit it back on but gave up.

James put down the book he was examining and came to look for himself. He tried to put the little drawer-face back. He put his fingers inside and there was a click. A panel sprung open and inside there was something wrapped in cloth. He lifted it out and unwrapped it to reveal a small key.

"Now, what do you suppose that's for?" he asked, turning it round in his hand. "It looks like it's off a jewellery box or maybe to wind a clock." He put it back and managed to fit the little drawer back into place.

The next room was a large sitting room, lavishly decorated in pale green and cream. There was a marble fireplace, set with paper wood and coals, just waiting for a match to set it alight. Above it hung a large painting, again with riders on horseback just like the wallpaper in the hall. Only, this time, they were galloping away from the chateau. I peeled back a dust sheet from one of the couches. They were upholstered in buttoned pale green velvet-like material, baby soft to touch. I sat down on one and ran my hand over the fabric.

"These are beautiful," Katie said, sitting down beside me, "and luxuriously comfortable. I love the lions' heads on the claw-like legs.

"There are so many contradictions here," I said. "The dust sheets, the packing cases, the neglected gardens, they all suggest they were leaving for good. Yet the fireplace is set to light and there is food in the kitchen, tins, boxes of coffee and tea and sugar, and biscuits with good, expired dates. It doesn't make sense."

Across the hall was a smaller sitting room, again with a fireplace waiting to be lit. On a little side table lay a newspaper that was three years old, an opened bottle of wine (half full), and two used wine glasses with dried up residue in their dusty glass.

"Come upstairs," James said. "There is something you need to see."

There were several bedrooms upstairs and the doors were all open except one. They were all beautiful and individually decorated. James went straight to the one closed door, opened it, and ushered us in. It was a child's room, decorated in pink. Toys lay in an open wicker hamper. A few stuffed dolls and furry animals sat on the bed and on shelves and there was also an empty photo frame on the dresser. The frame was silver with a tiny brightly enamelled Harlequin. Harlequins were my father's way of reminding me of Lanshoud and of the Wild hunt. He left them everywhere as a warning when an open gate to the other world was nearby. A shiver ran through me. I showed it to Katie who a moment later shivered too, as though it were contagious. The significance of that little figure was not lost on any of us.

James took a photograph from his pocket and handed it to me. "I took this photo from the frame when I was here last week. I intended to give it to you when I next saw you."

It was a family scene. A blond man and a woman with long red hair. The woman who held a blonde baby girl in a pink dress, was my mirror image. James said, "The woman in the photograph was obviously Elise, the man was Anton Bernard, and the child is their daughter Amandine. She is now five years old and has been in an orphanage since the accident."

"Amandine." I said her name whilst looking at her in the photograph. "It's a lovely name."

James stood, leaning against the dresser, watching our reaction to his bombshell revelation.

I passed the photograph to Katie. "Poor baby," she said. "She has lost both her parents and now she is in an orphanage."

I sat silent. James asked me, "What are you thinking?"

I looked up at him. "That I may be her next of kin," I said.

I had butterflies in my stomach, a mixture of excitement at the incredible thought that I could become a mother to this beautiful little girl, and the possibility that she may have relatives on her father's side. If so, they would be able to prove their relationship, whereas I could not. Yet, if there were other relatives, surely they would have claimed her by now. "James, would you be willing to help me find her?"

"I don't need to," he said. "I already know where she is. She has been in the Convent of St Martin orphanage near Epernay since the train crash."

"Epernay! The beautiful champagne town. I know it well. I have been there. Paul and I spent our last anniversary there, the year before he died. I don't remember seeing an orphanage."

"It's about one kilometre outside the town."

"Did you go to see it? How did you know where to start looking for her?"

"A friend in the DGIS put me in touch with a guy in the local gendarmerie. They were very helpful. They knew the house and the Bernard Family who lived here. In fact, one of them was a golfing friend of Anton. He actually offered to take me to the orphanage, but I made my own way there."

"Did you see Amandine?" I asked.

"No, they would not allow it, but I have spoken to the mother superior, and she has agreed to see you. I have told her you are the sister of Amandine's mother, but we have no documentary evidence of that. So, that photo you are holding is precious and may be enough for them to let you see Amandine from a distance.

"You have to prepare yourself for the fact that having the photo and the fact that you look like Elise, is not sufficient reason for them to hand Amandine over to you. Another thing you may want to consider is that seeing you might upset Amandine; if she was two at the time of the crash, she might recognise you and think you are her real mother. How traumatic would that be for her, when you then have to walk away?

"That photograph may be your ticket to at least discuss seeing her at a distance but be prepared; there is no guarantee that they will let you speak let alone even see her, so, just be glad the mother superior is willing to speak with you at all."

I sat still, shell-shocked, a little anxious but excited at the same time. Trying to take it in that there was a little girl, my niece, whom I could take and bring up and love and care for. I felt tears pricking my eyes. "When can we go? Will you take me there?" I asked.

James smiled. "I knew you would want to go soon so I have planned it all. They will contact me when an appointment is available. That could take weeks normally, but since you have travelled from Scotland, they have agreed to call me as soon as it becomes possible. Just don't build your hopes up."

We stopped off on the way back to the caravan park at the little café in Berny Riviere and had lunch. We had freshly caught fish, served with salad and there was a vast selection of pastries, to Katie's delight, but I struggled to eat anything. Excitement coupled with anxiety had ruined my appetite. Thoughts I knew were too stupid to even acknowledge were running through my head. What if someone adopted Amandine while I was impatiently waiting for an appointment just to see her?

Katie asked my opinion on something and then pointed out that I hadn't been listening to a word she said. She was right, of course, and was about to apologise when James's phone rang, and he answered and immediately smiled at me. He was speaking in fluent French. I understood enough to realise he was speaking to the convent. When the call ended, he said, "They have made allowances for the fact you have travelled a distance, so Mother Superior will see tomorrow at 11am."

Chapter Three

The Missing Child

Henri Picard, James' friend, the DGIS agent who traced Amandine to the convent, had offered to accompany us to the convent the next day. James believed Henri's credentials might open doors. Looking very serious, Katie had a couple of questions for James.

"Ok, what?" he asked.

She leaned across the table with a serious face and asked, "Henri, I like that name. Two questions: is he good-looking and is he married?"

James mused. "Is he married? Actually, I don't know. It never came up in conversation. He's never mentioned a wife. As for good-looking, I don't know what you would call good looking."

Katie groaned. "Just describe him – it's not difficult. Is he tall or short?"

James looked as though he was trying hard to remember, then said medium.

"Medium! What does that mean?"

James sighed then said a bit sharpish. "It means he is neither tall nor short." James frequently got fed up with Katie's continuous man hunt. "I don't know how tall he is. I didn't have a measuring tape on me when I met him."

I laughed and Katie glared at me. "James," she said, "this is serious. This guy could be the future love of my life. Observation and reporting back must be a good part of your job at MI5 or MI6 or whatever you are. Just describe him. It's not difficult.

What colour are his hair and his eyes? Just be serious for a moment!"

"Sorry, Katie," James said, wiping the grin off his face, and trying to look serious. He put his head back and closed his eyes. "Yes, I can see him," he said. "Henri's hair is dark, luscious and thick." He sighed deeply, "and when I look into his eyes, they are golden brown like a lion's. He has olive skin and rosy, red lips. He opened his eyes and grinned. "There does that help."

I couldn't help laughing and James was grinning again. Katie threw a napkin at him saying, "Oh you think you're so funny. You know, if I end up an old maid it will be partly your fault."

"Never," James said, "You will be swept off your feet someday. Someone will fall for those amazing curls, those soft brown eyes, and your endearing disposition."

"Flattery will get you nowhere, James Anderson, but keep going. I like it," Katie said smiling.

We sat on in that café at an outside table, enjoying the afternoon sunshine. Katie leaned over the table. "Hello." she said, snapping her fingers in front of my eyes. "Are you with us? Can you hear me?"

"Stop it," I pushed her hand away from my face. "What did you say?"

"I asked if you fancied a bit of shopping – there is a market on today – or are you too tired?"

"Yes, I am too tired."

Katie sighed. "I knew you were going to say that. That's not right, you know. It's not normal."

"What's not normal about being tired?" James asked.

Katie said "James, you need to be educated about women. Not wanting to shop is not normal. It is inherent in every woman's DNA to bargain hunt. Just hearing the words 'sale' or 'market' raises the blood pressure and heightens the hunting instinct.

Did you know that women on holiday can recognise the word sale in every language? Erica, however, seems to have a deficiency there. I've noticed it before. She has millions to spend yet she doesn't like shopping."

"Oh, now you are so funny, Katie," I said. "I was listening to you. I was just mesmerised watching that little girl over there. Look at her: she is absolutely gorgeous."

"I know, I've been watching you, watching her. I hope you're not thinking along the lines she could be Amandine?"

"No, don't be ridiculous. I know she couldn't be Amandine. She is too young for a start. Amandine will be five years old by now." I sighed, "I was just thinking how lovely It would be to have a little girl like that."

"I suppose," Katie said. "She is super cute, that little one. She's been very quiet. I think she has a kind of lost look about her."

The little girl who looked around three years old had left her mother's side and wandered over to us. She stood looking at the table. Katie was right: she had a kind of fey look about her, as though she didn't really know where she was. She was lovely, with her golden curls spilling out from under a floppy pink floral sun hat. Her plain, snowy white cotton dress, embroidered with flowers round the hem, was a little too long for her, reaching down almost to her white ankle socks and little pink sandals, with Peppa Pig faces on them. She looked like a doll straight off a toy shop shelf.

Katie and I both said "hello" to her and then "bonjour". She looked at us blankly with her big blue eyes then went back to staring at the table. In my pathetic classroom-level French, I asked her what her name was. She didn't answer.

Katie said, "She is like a doll."

"A doll who is after your dish of Marshmallows," James said smiling.

Her mother suddenly realised she was at our table and came over to apologise. I tried my school French again, successfully this time, asking the child's name.

"This is Chloe," her mother said, smiling. She spoke English and chatted to us for a little while, telling us that they were on holiday too, from Bordeaux. She allowed Chloe to have two marshmallows and told her to say thank you in English before taking her away.

The encounter with the child only made me even more excited about going to the orphanage the next day. I had a sleepless night, tossing and turning, thinking about the adoption, telling myself not to get excited as it may never come to anything. It must have been 5am before I finally fell asleep, and I awoke around eight, still tired, but looking forward to the day ahead.

I wandered into the kitchen area and, because the walls in the caravan were so thin, I could hear James speaking to someone in his bedroom. I was filling the kettle with fresh water when he came out with his mobile in hand. He said, "I didn't think you would be up yet."

"I know I couldn't get to sleep last night. I tossed and turned all night, all sorts of things going on in my head." Then I asked, "Did you sleep well?"

"Like a log," he said, putting his phone down on the table. He leaned over it, spreading his hands out, staring at it as though he expected it to ring again, which it did. He picked it up. After a minute, he groaned, "Ok, thanks Henri, thanks anyway."

"Do you want coffee?" I asked.

He didn't answer. He rubbed his eyes and ran a hand through his hair. A habit I recognised as something James did when he was stressed. His face told me something wasn't right.

I took a deep breath and asked,

"What is it? What's wrong?"

I waited while he was obviously choosing his words carefully before he delivered the blow and, when he did, my heart sank. "I'm afraid I have some bad news. That was Henri Picard, the guy who was taking us to the orphanage today."

"Was taking us! Past tense?" I asked, "Yes, I'm sorry Henri had to cancel."

"Why are you sorry? It's disappointing but it's not really a problem, is it? You have been there. You know where it is. We don't need him to take us."

"No, we don't, but Henri had a better chance of getting information. Anyway, it's more than that," he said.

I felt a wave of foreboding creeping over me. I said, "James if you have bad news, just spit it out." Every horrible possibility was creeping into my head: maybe they wouldn't let me see Amandine, or the appointment at the orphanage had been cancelled, or some relative on her father's side had already applied for adoption, or worse: something had happened to her."

"Just tell me," I almost shouted.

"He looked me straight in the eye and said very slowly, "There... is... no... orphanage."

"What! What do you mean there is no orphanage?"

"I mean just that. The building is now owned by a rich French businessman who deals in champagne. He used it for marketing, storage, and entertaining buyers. His business folded and now the building has been up for sale for at least a year."

Sinking onto the sofa I said, "I don't understand. Where are the children?"

"According to Henri, they were moved on. It had less than a handful of children living there and so it was closed down two years ago. There is no longer anyone living in that building."

"How can that be? You saw them just days ago, James. You spoke to them, didn't you?"

"Erica, I didn't see anyone. I wasn't inside the grounds – the gates were locked."

Confused, I said, "But you did speak to them."

James said, "Yes, I did, but it was on my mobile. The person I spoke to, told me to leave my number and they would arrange an appointment. When I took the call in the cafe yesterday, the woman who gave me the appointment told me to call back early in the morning and confirm it, as the mother superior was out. She said they had put it in her diary. It should not be a problem but it would be better if I called back in the morning to confirm. I did. I called this morning. The line was dead. I called the operator. She told me that number was not in use, and she had no other listed number for the convent." He lifted his mobile. "I called Henri and that was him calling back. When he traced Amandine to the convent orphanage, he had no idea it had closed two years ago."

"You didn't see anyone when you went? Any children? Anyone at all? Did you not think that was strange?"

"No, I didn't," he said. "There was torrential rain that day. I presumed they were all inside." What he said next sent a shiver down my spine. "I don't even know who, or what, I was speaking to when I called them or when I took their call back. Erica, that phoneline no longer exists; according to the exchange it has been disconnected for over a year." At this point Katie staggered out of her room, groggy and yawning. "What's going on? It's only eight o'clock, do you two never sleep?" She dropped down on the sofa. "Are you going to put that kettle on? I'll have coffee and stick some bread in the toaster for me please. I'm starving." She rubbed her eyes hard and looked up at us "Ok, what's wrong now? What is it this time?"

"You tell her," I said to James, while I sat down beside her. He did and she was as confused as I was. She put her arm around me, hugged me and said "I'm sorry. You must be so disappointed. Why is it every time you think things are going well, there's a massive u turn?"

James explained, "Henri, my contact at the DGIS who was taking us there, called me this morning. He apologised profusely for the information he had given about Amandine's whereabouts. He had just discovered the orphanage had closed down two years ago. The nuns, who were a British order, went back to the UK and the handful of children left in the orphanage were relocated to an SOS village about ten miles north from here. I'd never heard of SOS. villages. I looked them up online."

He scanned through his mobile and read out...

"SOS village are a world-wide organisation that set up homes for orphaned children. They are designed to give children a more family-centred home environment. In Europe, each house has only around six children of different ages and they have a house mother, sometimes a father too, and siblings. There are many of these houses in purpose-built villages around the world. They are built and designed to fulfil all the needs of the children – emotional, educational, and social."

He held up his phone.

"Amandine is in one of these villages and it just so happens it's not that far from here."

"How is that bad news at all?" Katie asked. "You know where she is now. Erica might even have a better chance of seeing her there."

"Yes and no," James said. "The problem is that we can't just walk into the village. It can take up to four weeks to get an appointment. There are rules and regulations about when and how you talk to the children they care for. Henri spoke to a colleague who was a sponsor. She read him the rules and then Henri emailed me a copy."

James handed me his mobile. It was a long list.

1. On your visit, you will be accompanied at all times by a member of staff.
2. You must present your passport or your I.D.
3. You are only allowed one visit per year, to ensure the daily routine of the child is not disturbed.

4. If you are a relative, plan your visit at least four weeks in advance, so that we may be sure the children are in the village and not on an outing and that they are prepared, informed and ready to meet you.

5. Do not invite children to be alone with you or to take part in activities outside the village. We are responsible for the children and will not allow it.

6. Do not speak to children about their past, their health conditions, or any sensitive information.

7. Obtain permission before taking photographs.

8. Do not share any personal information with the child or their village.

9. You must also declare if you have, at any time, been investigated for, or have been charged or convicted of, any crimes.

James added, "There is one suggestion Henri made. The international villages rely heavily on sponsorship and charitable donations. Erica, he suggested that you might want to consider giving a donation or sponsoring a child, as that might make your application move faster. He says he has printed out the application form and posted it to the campsite office for you."

"That's a great idea, Erica," Katie said. "Maybe you could sponsor Amandine. That's if she doesn't already have a sponsor, of course."

"Or I could make a large donation and that would sweeten my application."

"Either or," James said, "It's worth trying."

It was a lot to take in. I needed time to think. I said, "I'm going to walk down to the camp bakery and get some fresh orange juice and croissants."

"Would you like me to walk with you?" James asked. "No, I'm fine. I want to clear my head."

"Get some pastries for later," Katie called, as I closed the caravan door.

It was a beautiful morning. I took the long way to the camp bakery, but it was worth it, just to stroll through the small forest in early morning sunshine. A gentle breeze stirred the treetops, and the birds were singing their hearts out. It took twenty minutes longer to walk this way, because the path circled around the caravan park, but it was worth it.

Even though it would take time, a massive donation and sponsorship, it had to be the way forward. I was a multi-millionaire, so money was no object and, in my experience, money opened many doors far more resistant than that of a children's charity. I had a strong feeling it would work out. Suddenly, I heard footsteps behind me. I started to turn, thinking James had followed me when something hit me on the back of my head. I didn't even feel any pain, just a flash of bright white light and then everything went black.

When I woke up, everything was still black. I had a hood over my head and my wrists and ankles were strapped tightly together with what felt like duct tape. I was lying on a foul-smelling mattress in a vehicle, surrounded by the hollow sound of a large empty van. I tried pulling off the hood, but it was tied tightly behind my neck and, although I could reach it, I could only touch it with my fingertips. I would never be able to loosen it.

I sat up, panicking, gasping for breath, sucking in the cloth of the hood every time I inhaled. Yet I must have been breathing while I was unconscious, so there was air coming in from somewhere. I ran my fingers over the cloth and found the small hole that had been cut out over my mouth to let me breathe. I tried to tear it wider, but the material was too strong. It was hot inside the hood and the back of my neck was wet with blood. I remembered reading scalp wounds bleed profusely. Did that mean I could bleed to death? I started praying to every saint I knew to help me.

No one would be looking for me. Katie and James would presume I was held up in a queue at the bakery. It could be an hour before they thought to try looking for me. The van could have travelled a distance in that time – thirty, maybe forty miles or more, in any direction. My heart was thudding in my chest and I felt sick with fear.

There was a noise in the van – something rattling back and forth against the mattress. I felt along the side and, after a few attempts, finally caught it; it was a two inches long screw. If I could get the head into my mouth and grip it with my teeth then, maybe if I stabbed at it, I could burst the duct tape. Gripping it tightly in my fingers, I was nervous, anxious, and praying to God to help me.

With difficulty, I managed to sit up with my back against the metal wall of the van. I wiped the screw head on my white linen trousers and managed to put it through the hole in the mask and grip the head in my teeth. I had to do it, sore head or not. On my first try, the van went over a bump, my head hit the wall, and the head of the screw burst my gum, forcing me to drop it. Panicking at the passage of, and at the thought they could stop the van at any time, I searched frantically, telling myself that it would be there somewhere. Since it was not rolling about, it must have fallen on the mattress. I spat out blood and it dribbled down my chin inside the mask. It was salty, metallic, and disgusting.

It could have been worse: I could have swallowed it. Feeling along the mattress, inch by inch, I found the screw again. With it back between my bloodied teeth, gripping it hard, and after several tries, I poked the tape until the screw burst through. It took some force, and I punctured my wrist at the same time. Holding the screw tightly between my teeth I brought my wrists back and forth against the screw, poking more holes, in and out, in and out, stretching the holes each time.

My progress was slow because the duct tape was so strong. The cut on my wrist wasn't deep but, between that and the blood from my gum, the screw had become slippery. I had no way of putting pressure on it, so I let it bleed, cleaned the nail on my trousers every so often and kept going. I frequently missed the hole in the hood, when I was trying to spit blood through it. Instead, it ran down my chin and neck.

It was a long laborious task. Each time I punctured the duct tape I stretched my hands apart to make the hole bigger. On the edge of tears and about to give up, the tape burst open. Saying "thank you, God", I set to work, pulling the tape off. It was painful, taking some skin with it, but it was worth it. I undid the knot in my hood and pulled it off. I was free... except, I wasn't.

The bright sunlight streaming through the small windows in the van doors dazzled me. I looked out but could only see a quiet stretch of road, farmland and an occasional car. I didn't even try the lock. The last thing I needed was to fall out of the van. Looking around, I saw the van was not entirely empty. There was a blue metal box strapped to the wall near the doors. Maybe there was something in it I could use. Time was of the essence. I had to reach that toolbox before they stopped the van.

I was just in time as the van was already slowing down. It turned sharply right, and I fell – fortunately, it was back onto the mattress. I staggered up on jelly legs, almost losing my balance, but managed to reach the thankfully unlocked toolbox. It was a godsend, an Aladdin's treasure trove of heavy metal tools and just what I needed: there was a tyre iron.

I took it and closed the box. I staggered back and lay down on the mattress hiding the tyre iron between my legs. I then put my hood back on and settled down to wait, which was just as well because, at that point, the van turned a corner, slowed down to a crawl and then drew to a halt.

I closed my eyes and waited, the driver's door opened and then slammed shut. I listened carefully. There were no voices, which was good: I was praying he was on his own. There was a loud creaking sound of a gate being pushed open, then he got back in the van. He drove very slowly and then stopped, got out again and slammed the van door shut. Again, there were no voices.

He unlocked and opened the back doors of the van. I froze, listening to him huffing and puffing, realising he must be overweight because he was struggling to pull himself into the van. That was good; it meant, if I had to, I could outrun him.

I kept my hands and feet close together. The tyre iron jammed between my legs. He thought I was still unconscious because, grunting with effort, he dragged the mattress feet first to the door, cursing as he struggled – not in French but, to my horror, in German.

Another wave of panic gripped me as I realised it had to be Die Bruder. They were behind this! He was bringing me to them. I had to act now. The sun was streaming through the open van doors, allowing me to see his shape through the material of the hood. He was backing himself down the steps, so it was now or never. If I fell into their hands, I would die… or worse, I would be tortured until they got the keys to the gates and access to the wormholes. I sat up and swung the tyre iron with all my might. It must have cracked his skull because he dropped like a stone.

Watching him in case he moved, shaking like a leaf, my legs like jelly, I climbed over him. All the time, I was expecting him to wake, wielding my blood-stained tyre iron ready to strike again. My intention was to run. Instead, I stood, shaking and dumbstruck: I was standing in front of Chateau Langedechu.

My mind was in turmoil, my instinct was to run and keep running, but I knew there was a vast forest around Langedechu; there was nowhere to run too. What if Die Bruder were in the chateau? They could be watching and coming for me as that very moment. I was panicking, shaking. I took deep breaths. There was no movement from the greasy, foul-smelling heap at my feet. Then I saw them, the van keys in his hands. I grabbed them I had to drive that van now before anyone appeared from the house.

My hands were so shaky I couldn't get the key in the ignition. It was of course a left-hand drive, but it didn't matter. I didn't even stop to put the seat belt on; I just had to get away from there. The engine started at the first turn of the ignition. I took off, driving fast and with only one thought – to get away. I took the turn too quickly, skidded and slammed sideways into the big gates at the end of the driveway. I was lucky it was sideways; the impact could have catapulted me through the windscreen. I pulled my seatbelt on, not stopping to see if I was being followed. I just put my foot on the accelerator and kept going.

Suddenly, I was out on the road. I had no idea in what direction to go – I just drove. I had my wits about me enough to at least stay on the right-hand side of the road. I had no idea which direction I was going in. I was just trying to get as far away as possible. I passed two cottages, too afraid to stop. Die Bruder might be in them – two cars passed. I couldn't flag them down for help: what if some of the Die Brueder were in one those cars?

I kept going until it led onto a motorway. It was wide and open, and I pushed the accelerator to get as far away as I could. Another panic. The fuel gauge! I hadn't checked the fuel gauge but, to my relief, it was still half full. I drove for an hour along an endless motorway, not recognising any of the risk signs. I had just decided to stop at the next village or garage or anywhere there was people who could help me.

Then I heard it, music to my ears, a police siren. They waved me over to the hard shoulder and pulled in behind me. When the officer opened the door of the van, I burst into tears. They questioned me and one of the officers spoke enough English to understand I had been kidnapped. They put me in the back of the police car, giving me a box of tissues and a bottled water. The older man, who spoke English, said they were taking me to a hospital first to have my injuries treated. I told him I was fine. I just wanted to go back to the caravan park. He said it was procedure: the hospital for a check-up then the police station. James and Katie would be worried by now and would no doubt have contacted the police.

The older man asked if I had a contact number. I had no mobile and I didn't know Katie's or James's mobile number by heart; all I ever did was look up their name on my mobile. I told him the name of the caravan park and the number of the caravan.

I asked what time it was, he said, "It is seven in the evening. Don't worry: these camp offices are open until late."

By 7pm, I had been missing for thirteen hours. Katie and James would be frantic. The older man stepped outside the car and made a call on his mobile. I couldn't hear what he was saying, and I would not have understood his French anyway. He got back in the car smiling. "A car will be sent for your friends, and they will meet us at the hospital."

The police car pulled back onto the road and turned around at the next junction. Exhaustion and the heat in the car overwhelmed me, and I fell asleep. I only awoke again when the car slowed and went over a bumpy road. It looked familiar. Then terror gripped me, this was no hospital. They had brought me back to Langedechu. The younger officer opened the door, grabbed my arm, and pulled me out. I was dizzy, nauseated, and I started retching before vomiting over him. He pushed me away and I fell. He was leaning over me shouting and cursing in German.

Chapter Four

Escape From the Chateau

The younger officer took charge. He tied my arms behind my back and pushed me forward up the stairs and into the hall of the chateau, where there was a woman waiting. She was a big, big woman, built like a man, or she may have been a man dressed as a woman. It was hard to tell. The creature had a man's haircut and a face that my adopted Scots mother would have described as looking like the backend of a bus.

I call her a woman as she was dressed in a white shirt and a straight no-nonsense knee length black skirt. She spoke sharply to the man in German and pulled my arm again, forcing me to follow her upstairs. "In there," she said as she pushed me into a bedroom. Her English was good, but she was definitely German.

It was a simple room with a single bed and a table, nothing like the luxury of the rooms I had seen when I came here with James and Katie. It was on a mezzanine level, with the window overlooking the side of the house. It may have been a maid's room. It was dusty and cold, and I was shivering. There was duct tape around my wrists. I had conquered that before and I could do it again. However, it was more difficult this time because he had tied my hands at the back. So, even if I had my trusty screwnail, it would have been no use. There wasn't even anything I could use to burst the tape – it was a bare room except for a bed and a small table – so I just lay down on the bed. There was no way to lay down comfortably without putting stress on my shoulders or twisting my neck. In spite of that, exhaustion sent me to sleep.

The door opening woke me. I was aching in every muscle in my body. It was the woman. She had a small bottle of water and a packet of biscuits in one hand and a pair of black patent stiletto shoes in the other. Draped over her arm, she had a vivid green silk evening dress. She told me to sit up and cut the tape on my wrists.

"Drink," she ordered, handing me the water bottle. I sat up, rubbing my aching shoulders. "Drink," she ordered again. I tried to hold the bottle, but the tape had been so tight I had almost lost the feeling in my hands – they were weak and trembling, I almost dropped it. She caught it and rammed it into my mouth, squeezing it in, choking me with the water.

"You will wash and wear this dress and these shoes," she spat at me, adding something in her guttural German accent that sounded like she was calling me a whore. "You are to dine with Herr Hoffmann this evening," she said, putting the dress on the bed.

"Who is he?" I asked.

"No questions," she said, holding a fist in my face. "You do what you are told."

The next hour was one of the worst in my life. She dragged me off the bed pulling me by my tee shirt to the door. In the hall, she kept pushing me along until I reached a bathroom. "In there," she said, "you will wash and be clean." She stepped in after me and closed and locked the door behind her.

"I need to use the toilet," I said, expecting her to leave, but she just pointed to the pan and folded her arms. With my bladder at bursting point, I had no choice.

I flushed the toilet and stood up. She came in very close, towering above me like an ogre "Take off your clothes," she said. I refused. She told me to strip, or I would lose my teeth. There was enough venom in her tone to make me believe her. I was sure she meant it.

She turned on the shower, pushing me in and blocking my attempt to close the door. She watched me shower. When I turned the tap off, she held out a bath towel saying, "I will help you dry."

"I don't need help," I said, reaching for the towel but she just laughed lifting it away.

Wrapping the towel around me, she started drying me slowly from the front. My skin was crawling with disgust. She was gazing into my eyes when I gathered as much spit as I could and shot it straight into her eyes. Bullseye! It caught her by surprise, she staggered back swearing in German. I threw myself at her, losing my balance, knocking her over and she fell back cracking her head on the tiled floor. I landed naked on top of the filthy bitch. Horrified and panicking, I tried to get away until I realised I had knocked her out.

There was a choice, dirty trousers, blood splattered tee shirt from my burst lip, and dirty white soft trainers or, the green silk dress, all of which lay on the floor. I watched the ogre closely for any sign of movement. She didn't stir. My hair soaking wet, my skin still damp, I pulled on my clothes – at least it was my own blood on them. I took the dress too, thinking it might be useful.

Opening the bathroom door, my heart pounding like a drum, I crept out. Looking back, I saw the gun that had fallen from her hand. I went back and grabbed it.

There were faint voices downstairs. Tiptoeing back to the bedroom, I realised that if I had any chance of escape it would have to be now and not down those stairs. I made it back to the room and locked the door. The gun in my hand gave me a sense of security; it was a godsend, as was the fact that I had been taught how to use one before the battle at Lanshoud.

There was a sash window in the room, and it opened easily but noisily. I held my breath. Any sound could be heard by everyone below, but there was nothing but loud voices and laughter from inside the house.

There was a broad decorative ledge underneath the window that ran around the building because it was on the mezzanine level. It was not too much of a drop, if I could somehow climb down. Knotted bed sheets came to mind, but there was nothing to tie them on to, and there may have been a window below this one, though I couldn't remember seeing one when I had walked around the chateau with James and Katie.

Nature was on my side; on the right-hand side, past another window, there was an enormous fir tree. It had been a Christmas tree at some point in its life, but now it was neglected; it had grown tall and strong and had reached the top of the chateau. Looking along the ledge towards the branches of the tree, I could see some of them were crossed – bonus! They would be even stronger. If it hadn't been so neglected and overgrown, I could not have reached it from the window but thankfully I could.

This should be easy for me. When I was young, I was always in trouble for climbing trees with my best friends, who were the twin boys that lived next door. My adopted Dutch father taught us all how to safely climb trees. He taught us to always look for something safer than just a branch to stand on. Instead, look for a knot in a branch or crossing branches. Well, I had that. I could see a platform created by the crossing branches from the window. We had to assess whether the branches could take our weight. I would do that. We had to make sure we always had three points of contact at any time. Two feet and one hand or two hands and one foot. He said, "Make sure you have your three points of contact at all times. Reach the trunk as fast as you can and stick to it as much as you can, keeping upright as much as possible. Keep an eye open for whose home you may be invading. Birds, squirrels, spiders, bugs etc. could fly in your face and make you lose your balance."

We were like monkeys back in those days: fearless and always in trouble for climbing. That was many years ago. Now the daredevil recklessness of childhood was long gone, but the skill was still there. I had all that ingrained into my brain. I could do it. I could climb that tree.

Just before I climbed out, I realised that, if they came looking for me, and the door was locked, they would break in and look to see if I had fled out the window. If I left the door open, they would think I was still in the house. I unlocked the door and checked there was still no movement outside. I didn't even know or care if the ogre was dead or alive. It was now or never.

I put the biscuits and water-bottle and handgun into the green dress and tied it round my waist, leaving my hands free. It was heavy and bulky but I managed it. Closing the window was tricky but I managed that too, making less noise than I had when I opened it. Finally, on the ledge it was now just one step at a time. The stone ledge was a decorative broad one or I would never have managed it at all.

Helpful was the very old and very strong honeysuckle hedge, intertwined with a vine of some sort, before growing together up the wall. They gave me something to hold onto. They would never take my weight but mentally it helped.

Without looking down I slowly made my way to the other window praying there was no one in that room. I peeped in but, thankfully, it was just a storeroom. Clinging to the honeysuckle and vine, I carefully moved along the edge, looking down every other moment to make sure there was no one there. I finally reached the tree's stout branches and there it was, the exact point where two branches crossed creating a platform.

Holding my breath, I reached over before edging out one foot, keeping to the rule of three. Scarily the branches swayed a little with every movement I made, but I felt safe enough crawling along to reach the trunk. Thankfully, the tree was bushy and easy to hide in. Climbing slowly and carefully, testing each branch before climbing onto it, my heart was thudding in my chest. I climbed as far as I could, until I felt the branches became too small to support me. Finally, and gratefully, I settled with my back against the trunk and sighed with relief: I had made it.

I started trembling and burst into tears. I had been through much worse than this over the past few years, but I was never as alone as I felt at that moment. I managed to pull myself together by reminding myself that there was one thing I could guarantee, and that was that the people I loved most in this world would stop at nothing until they found me.

My plan was to wait until nightfall and then sneak down the tree. I settled down and ate some of the plain digestive biscuits and drank some of the water left in the bottle, but not too much: I could be quite a while up this tree. I pulled the green dress over my tee shirt; it was perfect camouflage, being that it was the exact same shade of green as the tree. Now it was just a case of waiting until nightfall to climb down.

I checked out the gun. It was lightweight, the kind a woman would use, even though it was fully loaded. I felt safer with it in my hand. Thank God the angels had taught me how to use one before the attack at Lanshoud. I knew I would use this gun if I had to. I may have already killed the guy that kidnapped me in the van and now, for all I knew, the ogre on the bathroom floor in the chateau could be dead too. Still, I had no intention of finding out.

Before long, there was a commotion at the door of the house. A lot of shouting and lots of movement. People running. A car engine started and took off. It was impossible to see anything through the thick network of branches, which at least meant they couldn't see me. I sat still, not wanting to risk any movement for hours on end, even when it was obvious they had given up trying to find me.

I was tired, but the afternoon nap, tied up on the bed, had helped me not to fall asleep on the tree and the night itself was anything but silent. Owls hooted to one another, foxes barked, the leaves above me rustled. Something was running through the trees behind the house and screeching. I almost fell asleep just before dawn broke. It was cold though there was no wind. All was silent and it was time to move. I ate the last biscuit, took the last sip of water and jammed the bottle against the trunk between branches.

The dress was a nuisance, getting snagged on branches, but I needed it for camouflage. I tucked as much of it as I could inside my trousers and put the gun in my belt. It was scary going down; branches shivered, bristled, and crackled with every movement.

Pausing every few seconds to listen, I finally made it to the lower branches that were bigger, stronger, and flexible enough for me to swing down onto the ground without snapping.

My plan was to get as far away from the house as I could. Not by the road but through the trees at the back of the chateau. There was an eerie mist in my favour. Still, I had to move fast while it gave me some cover, hopefully concealing me from anyone looking out from a window. I didn't stop to check. I just ran, not down the driveway, going around the back of the house and through the gardens there. Running on grass instead of paths, worried as I was that they would hear the movement of stone chips on the path. I had no idea what or if anything other than fields or forest lay there. When I looked back, there were lights on in windows at the rear of the house. They could be after me soon.

It was cold and there was a dampness in the air. The morning sun was struggling to pierce, never mind disperse, the grey/white mist. This was a dense forest. It was dark and creepily silent. The sun was rising and, with trees as far as the eye could see, there should have been a dawn chorus, but the birds were silent. I walked on, gun in hand, until I heard the crackle of bushes behind me. Something was there; my heart was racing. It might just be an animal, a deer maybe. I wondered they have wolves here in this part of France. I stood stock still, holding my breath, the gun ready. It was only a deer, a gentle doe-eyed creature. We stared at each other, both of us reluctant to move, then there was another crackle in the bushes that startled her, and she ran off.

The mist was still lingering but I could see ahead. The trees ended with a fenced off field, full of sheep. Walking slowly, hoping not to spook them, and start them running, I managed to reach the other side of the field first. I was in among trees again and, before long, I heard the sheep running and bleating loudly. I could hear voices shouting too. Then I saw them, three men in among the sheep. I could hear their voices calling to each other. There was a clearing in front and a path. I could see the shape of buildings.

I could get help. I climbed over the fence and straight into a cemetery. There was nothing but gravestones as far as the eye could see.

It wasn't a little graveyard – it was more like a cemetery belonging to a town or that you would find in a city. I ran along a path as fast as I could. The men were close behind. I could hear the sheep still kicking up a fuss at the invasion of their field. I had to find somewhere to hide.

Running through the cemetery, past multiple gravestones, I came onto a path. It was lined with large monuments and ornately gated tombs. In the middle of the row was the largest tomb of all. Above its stone entrance stood the statue from which Langedechu got its name. The statue of the Fallen Angel. The angel was larger than life, although it was exactly the same as the painting in the chateau.

The whole monument was surrounded by white railings, the paint weathered and chipped. The gates lay open and there was a metal door that sat directly under the feet of the angel. It was lying slightly open, just enough to let me see the dark interior and steps going down. I turned, ready to run, when a voice called softly, "Erica."

Coming from the tomb, the sound was horrible; I almost lost the contents of my bladder. I froze. The quiet voice called again, "Erica, come here. Don't be afraid." The voice was coming from the stairs, from the dark. It was black as coal in there. It whispered again, "Erica."

I turned to run away but my legs wouldn't move. I was now completely frozen with fear; my feet were paralysed. I even hoped the Germans would appear. Suddenly, a hand clamped over my mouth and dragged me backwards through the open door.

"Hush, my dear," the voice hissed in my ear. Then I was half lifted and carried down the stairs into the pitch-black darkness of the tomb, at which point I passed out.

I woke up to find I was lying on a stone floor wrapped in what felt like a jacket. It was as silent as the grave. I didn't know where I was. Shakily, I stood up and stretched out my hand but couldn't even feel a wall. There was a noise, a scratching, like a mouse or a rat, which made me frightened to move. I held my breath. Silence.

There was a glimmer of light above me and to my horror I saw it was the top of the stairs and the open metal door. I was in the tomb. Someone had dragged me down there. Was it to save me from the men who were chasing me? Or was it for something much worse? Who had wrapped me in this jacket?

I wanted to ask if there was someone there, but I was equally terrified that someone, or worse, something, would answer me. I had to get up those stairs. I had to get out of there.

I pulled the jacket on and walked towards the light, waving my hand in front of me. I couldn't see anything but the top of the stairs. Shaking, I found it difficult to keep my balance because I didn't want to reach out and actually touch something. I tripped and fell on the bottom step, resulting in a very painful cut on my shin. Oddly, that pain helped me to pull myself together.

I made it up and out of the door, staggering into the now bright sunshine and cold fresh wind. So terrified was I of what lay below, I would have been happy to find the Germans outside waiting for me, but there was no one there. The whole cemetery was as silent as the tomb. It was empty of the living, not even the twitter of a bird.

I hurried away on jelly legs to the end of the row of tombs. Looking towards the houses I had seen before, I saw that there were more trees, if I could get through them, I would reach the houses. Only halfway there, exhaustion hit me. There was a fallen tree so, feeling really weak, I sat down on it.

The jacket was keeping me warm. It was a big man's jacket. The shoulders were halfway down my arms, and I had to crunch up the sleeves to put my hands in the pockets. When I did, there was a pleasant surprise. Tangerines and a biscuit.

Whose jacket was this? Who had rescued me and left me in the tomb? Who had left two tangerines and a biscuit in the pockets? Were they left for me? I wolfed them down anyway. Taking the jacket off and searching it, there was nothing in the jacket to identify the owner. The label was a well-known Italian designer, so no clue there.

It was important to keep moving, so gathering as much willpower as I could, I made it through the trees and ended up before the rear fence of a row of houses. There was an elderly woman in the garden, hanging out washing. Deaf as a doornail, she didn't hear me calling to her. I lifted a little stone and threw it near her. She didn't see or hear it. I was desperate so, I hit her with the next one. It was only a pebble really, yet she shrieked as though it had been a rock and ran shouting into the house. That brought out not only her husband but the man next door too.

"Gendarme," I pleaded. I put my hand to my ear mimicking a phone call and repeated "gendarme," asking them to call the police.

The woman's husband opened the gate, he and the neighbour ushered me into the garden. They studied me. The woman looked me up and down and immediately became suspicious. "Gitane," she said, spitting out the word. She waved her hand frantically, shooing me back out of the gate. I dropped to my knees, more with weakness than anything else. Begging her to help me, I pleaded with her, my hand at my ear mimicking a phone, "Madam, s 'il vous plait, gendarme."

The woman hesitated, she studied me, my green dress ripped, the blood on my leg, she rattled something about the gendarme to her husband, calling him Albert. Her husband shrugged. The men were not friendly. I learned later gitane meant gypsy. She was telling them to get rid of me and so the husband Albert was about to pull me to my feet but the neighbour, who was staring at me, studying me in a peculiar fashion, caught his arm and said something quietly that stopped him. In fact, he looked stunned. Albert put on his spectacles and they both looked at me more closely. "Mon Dieu!" Albert exclaimed.

The wife, who was called Marie, grunted, and grabbed my arm and pulled me to my feet, dragging me towards the gate again, the neighbour, Gaston, was bizarrely smiling at me and rattled out in French something that sounded like sympathy, to the annoyance of Marie, who had had enough. She was about to throw me out when Albert suddenly cried out, he closed the gate, crying "no, no, no, Marie, elle n'est pas une gitane." He was telling her I was not a gypsy.

He turned to his neighbour, Gaston, and said something quietly to him that sent them both nodding their heads in agreement. Still, they acted strangely, as though something had excited them. The husband gently put his hand on my arm, waving his wife out of his way. He took me into their home and sat me gently on the sofa. It was such a sudden change of heart I was completely confused, grateful but confused.

Albert put his hand to his ear, mimicking a phone call, shaking his head, and pointing to the door saying, "Gaston" and "gendarme". He was telling me their phone wasn't working, and the neighbour was calling the police.

He asked me some questions. I decided it was best not to speak at all. I just repeated the mimicking of phone at my ear saying, "Gendarme."

Now Marie was weirdly smiling at me too and patting my arm. Bewildered by their reaction, I tried to understand what they were quietly whispering to each other, as Marie's attitude had changed so quickly from hostility to concern. In fact, she was now all over me like a rash, shooing her husband away and bringing me a glass of home-made lemonade. There was no point in asking why. The husband, Albert, and his neighbour, Gaston, were calling the police and that was all that mattered.

As soon as the door closed behind Albert, his wife turned into a mother hen. She led me to a bathroom and gave me some clothes and a carrier bag to put my clothes in. Strangely, she was now addressing me as Madam.

It wasn't long before her husband came back. He was shouting at her. I picked up enough to realise he was berating her for letting me wash and for handling my clothes. I think he was accusing her of damaging important evidence. I wondered if he thought I had been attacked or raped or something. Then he said something that made them both smile. Suddenly it all became clear. His sentence contained a few words I recognized: "Langedechu" and "Madam Bernard". They thought I was Elise,

The local police were obviously not in a hurry. It was nearly two hours before they turned up. I learned later Gaston had worked at Langedechu a few years ago. He gave the police a description of the woman who had appeared at his neighbour's gate and told them that she was Elise Bernard, from Chateau Langedechu, whose body and not been recovered after the fatal train crash.

Such was the delivery of Marie's compassion and her determination to help me that, by the time the police arrived, I was washed and fed. In fact, I was also dressed in a black floral cotton dress, four sizes too big, and a large beige home knitted jumper that could have wrapped around me twice. I think Marie may have knitted it for her husband, as the arms reached my knees. However, the clothes were clean and warm, and I fell asleep on the sofa. Marie had tried asking me questions. I just looked at her blankly each time. Sitting in that bath a thought had dawned on me, a thought that triggered a shiver of excitement. What a chance had come my way. It was crazy, I knew, but if I could pull it off... If I didn't speak, it would give me time to think. If I could pass myself of as Elise, I could claim Amandine without all the red tape of adoption.

Sitting in the police car on the way to the station. I closed my eyes: I was daydreaming, escaping the horrors of the last few days. I could see myself claiming Langedechu and Amandine. Taking Amandine shopping, tucking her up in bed at night with a story.

Spoiling her with toys and clothes. The car slowed down, and I could hear a growing clamour of voices.

The driver slowed to a crawl as he tried to make his way through a horde of journalists flashing cameras. They were banging on the windows of the police car, Shouting, "Elise. Elise du Sante. Madam Bernard."

The driver gave a few blasts of the siren and crept forward through the crowd. Some police officers ran out the station, controlling the press, pushing them back, clearing the way to allow the car through. They locked the gates behind us. Two officers stood by, threatening anyone who tried to climb them.

A cloth was put over my head and face and I was rushed inside the station. Someone caught my arm, pulled the cloth off and said, "You idiot! What the hell are you playing at? Have you had a bang on your head or something? What made you think you could get away with lying to the French police?"

I was looking into the eyes of a very angry / relieved James.

Chapter Five

Paris and Henri

Later that afternoon, Katie and I (and our suitcases) were ensconced in a safe house in Paris. It was not what I expected, which was the kind of safe houses you see in TV crime dramas, cheap flats, sparsely furnished, temporary holding places for witnesses. Instead, it was a four bedroomed lavishly furnished apartment in a beautiful old building with balconies overlooking the Seine. It even had a tiny little elevator that was as old as the building. It had a door with a small glass window that opened onto a cage-like elevator and was so small that we just managed to squeeze the three of us and the luggage in and no more.

James pushed the buttons and cranked a handle on the side of the cage to make it work. The advantage of being in a cage was that we could see the landings and doors as we passed, so it was not as claustrophobic as it might have been. As we went up, I noticed there were only two doors on each floor. The elevator creaked and crawled at a snail's pace then it ground to a halt. We had reached the top. On this floor, there was only one door.

James tried to open the cage, but it was stuck. He pulled the metal concertina door, then he pushed all the buttons over and over – but nothing worked, neither the red emergency button nor the elevator telephone. The gate just wouldn't budge. We all tried our mobiles but, of course, there were no signals on any of them.

"We could just shout for help," Katie said.

"No," James said sharply. "We don't want to draw attention. Henri is on his way. He will be here soon."

We were stuck in that elevator for around a half hour, although it felt like two hours. Katie and I sat on our cases. While James stood randomly pushing buttons.

Katie mused, "You know, I've seen plenty of safe houses on TV, but this building looks far too posh for that."

James answered, "It isn't that kind of safe house, as in a house owned by the police. Henri inherited this apartment when his parents died. Henri very kindly offered it for you as a safe place for you to stay while in Paris. You will like it. It's a really nice four-bedroom apartment. The building was built in 1930 and was damaged but managed to survive the bombing during the war. Henri has spent thousands renovating it."

"Oh, I am sure we will love it," Katie grunted. "That is, of course, if we ever get out of here."

A door opened and closed on the floor below us. The elevator jerked, rattled and started to descend. It stopped and the doors opened on an elderly lady with a walking stick. We got out with our cases. James had a conversation with her in French, which I understood most of. He was telling her not to use the lift as it was not working, and we had been trapped in it for nearly an hour. Just a little exaggeration.

She was very sympathetic and smiling, but as she walked past him into the lift, she was rattling away in French, pointing to the handle, holding up three fingers and saying something three times. We discovered she was telling him that, when it was stuck, he had to crank it three times. She then looked at our cases, wished us a happy holiday, cranked the handle three times, pushed the button and down it went.

James and I took the elevator with the cases back up to the fourth floor. Katie in a mood, took the stairs.

Henri's apartment was stunning. Lavishly furnished, with floor to ceiling windows and a small veranda at the front with a view of the river. James opened the door on a large bedroom with twin beds and an en-suite bathroom. "Will this do?" he asked, knowing full well we would love it.

The bedroom was decorated in pale blue and silver. "Oh my God," Katie said, dropping onto one of the beds. "It's like lying on a cloud." She sighed and closed her eyes. "Wake me when dinner is ready, please. I feel traumatised and need some rest."

We shut the door on her.

I followed James into the kitchen, He seemed to know where everything was. He took out mugs and asked me to get the milk from the large American-style fridge, which was stocked with enough food to feed an army. He made tea for me and coffee for himself, then he sat opposite me at the table."

"I am very grateful to Henri for letting us stay here," I said. "Do you have any idea when we will be able to leave?" He pushed his chair back and looked me straight in the eye. He was obviously not happy.

"Leave! Leave for where? Where exactly are you planning to go? Has it slipped your mind that you confessed to the French police to possibly having killed two people, whose bodies, by the way, haven't been found? Or that you told them you had been kidnapped by Germans who were also nowhere to be found. Then you tried to pass yourself off as the missing Elise Bernard! What part of your brain thought that was all right?

"Do you know what I think? You were damned lucky Erica. You have a lot more than hospitality to thank Henri for."

Henri arrived about 4.30pm that afternoon. He was not what I had expected and certainly not what James had led Katie to believe. He was, I thought, in his late fifties, as he had greying hair, and wore gold-rimmed wire-like spectacles. He looked tired and worn in a way that belied the character and brilliant mind we were soon to be familiar with.

"Erica Cameron, we meet at last. I have heard so much about you from James. May I call you Erica? I am so pleased to meet you." He came over and gave me a peck on both cheeks. "And this is Katie, I presume?" he said, kissing a delighted Katie on both cheeks. "I hope James has made you both comfortable."

"Yes, thank you," Katie said. "We are so much more comfortable here than in the caravan and we are both very grateful Monsieur Picard."

"Henri, please," he said.

"Henri," I said. "I am very grateful for your intervention at the police station. James assures me that you went to a lot of trouble, and he said, if it were not for you, I would be languishing in a cell right now instead of being a guest in your lovely home."

Henri laughed. "James exaggerates. It was no trouble." He put a tray with a bottle of red wine and five glasses on the coffee table. He poured out four and said, "Malbec, French of course; it is so much smoother than the Argentinian."

He settled back in his chair sipping the wine. "I have some important news for you, Erica. I am sorry to tell you. The police have searched the chateau and the estate with tracker dogs. I am afraid they found no evidence of anyone having been there. There was no body in the bathroom, as you had described. Neither was there any van, nor the body of the man you said you hit with the tyre iron. I am sorry, Erica, but there was nothing to corroborate any part of the statement you gave at the police station."

"Well, that's a blessing," Katie said. "At least they can't charge you with murder."

I was stunned. "How can that be?"

I felt my anxiety building up. I had butterflies in my stomach. I looked to James for support, but he was silent. He didn't even look up; he was just staring into his wine glass. I was devastated.

"How is that possible? There were at least five men in that house. I heard them talking and laughing and I saw them when I was hiding in the tree, when they came out of the house looking for me."

James and Henri remained silent.

I said, "As for the woman I pushed in the bathroom, she said I was to dine with a man she called Herr Hoffman. When I pushed her, and she fell and hit her head on the tiles, she wasn't moving. I was afraid I had killed her. If there was no blood on the tiles, at least there must have been fingerprints."

James looked up. "There were fingerprints in the bathroom and in the room you slept in that were an identical match to yours taken at the police station. There were no other prints."

Katie said, "How can there be no other fingerprints? If nothing else, we must have left prints on the day you took us to the chateau. We touched lots of things that day."

Henri said, "There were no other fingerprints anywhere in the house. The forensic team were thorough. Everything, with the exception of those two rooms, the bathroom, and the bedroom you were in, is covered in dust."

"What about the green dress, the woman told Erica to wear?" Katie asked.

"Katie's right," I said. "The German woman's fingerprints will be on that dress. She handed it to me and told me to wear it. The elderly woman took the dress and gave me her clothes to wear. She may still have the dress. The German woman's fingerprints will be on that."

James shook his head. "Clothing is a poor option for fingerprints. It depends on the material, but they generally don't last long on fabric unless it's smooth like leather. If the material is porous, empty spaces won't retain the pattern of the fingerprint. Even creases in material can interfere with a print. No, even if the forensics team got prints from the dress, they would have been disturbed by way too many outside influences, too many people handling it. There is no proof they committed any crime."

That evening, Henri cooked us a delicious meal. We sat around the table chatting. He had such a calm, gentle, fatherly tone to his voice and, with his French accent, it was as soothing as silk to the ears. I could have listened to him all day.

"Erica, may I ask you some questions?"

"Yes, of course."

"Thank you. I am sure you realise James has told me your story. Forgive me please, but I must describe it as incredible, a story of gates and keys and time travelling…" He chuckled. "Were it from someone else's mouth I would have dismissed it as lunacy, but I know James – he and I go back a long way. I know he does not suffer fools gladly and so I have an open mind, and I am very interested in your story. I am afraid I will have a lot of questions to ask you, and you must forgive me, my English it is not perfect."

"It's a lot better than her French," James muttered under his breath. "Not that it stopped her from trying to pass herself off as being French. Honestly, Erica, I have seen you take risks but lying to the police, pretending to be a missing person, is a whole new level of stupidity. As far as the French police are concerned, Elise is not dead. She is missing, presumed dead. Did you even consider for one moment that Elise may have survived that crash? That she may be out there somewhere and that you passing yourself off as her might stop the authorities from looking for her. It was not only stupid it was selfish too."

If there was one thing I hated about James Anderson, it was that he often treated me like a child. He had the knack of making me feel like an idiot.

Henri stopped him. "Come James, eat. It will improve your mood. I think Erica and Katie have had enough stress for one day. Anyway, I have a surprise for you."

We gathered around the table. At that point, the door opened, and a girl's voice called out, "Bon soir, c'est moi."

"Of course, it is you," Henri called out. "Late as usual and, English please, remember I have guests. She walked into the dining room. She was beautiful, tall and slim with shining black hair, tied back into a chignon, she was dressed in a blue tailored suit and stilettos that looked as though she had just walked off the catwalk.

James immediately stood up, pushed back his chair, held out his arms and cried, "Marianne! Is it really you? What a lovely surprise." He held her at arm's length, looked her up and down and said, "You look amazing."

Unfortunately, he was telling the truth. Marianne threw her arms around his neck and kissed him on both cheeks. "James, darling, I cannot believe you are here. It has been so long," she purred.

"Too long," James said.

"Put him down, Marianne," Henri called. "Come and sit with my guests. Let me introduce you to Erica and Katie."

"Forgive me please," she said. "It has been such a long time since I have seen James." She flashed a smile at him. "We were once, how you would say, an item."

Henri pulled out a chair for her. "Give me your jacket and sit down. I am trying to serve dinner. Erica, Katie, may I introduce my little sister, Marianne."

Marianne Picard was one of these people you could never forget. She was captivating and vivacious and would always be the centre of attention. She lavished all her attention on James that night, encouraging him to share amusing stories from the times they had spent together.

James was definitely uncomfortable, but he went along with it. She would tell a story and then encourage James to add to it. Then, fuelled by the wine, they would end up helpless with laughter.

When dinner was over, and we had moved to the comfortable living room, Marianne and James shared one of the sofas. The only thing they didn't do was hold hands. Marianne, with wine glass in hand, suddenly asked me if I would tell her, bit by bit, what had happened at Langedechu.

Heaven knows why, but I was immediately annoyed. It must have showed on my face that I felt it was none of her business. Worse, Katie jumped in with, "Erica's tired. I think she has had enough questions for one day." It wasn't even what she said, it was the aggressive 'I don't like your tone,' it was delivered in, that made me cringe. Not that it upset Marianne, she was either oblivious or just didn't give a damn.

I hesitated. Henri picked up on my reluctance and said, "Erica, let me reassure you that you can tell Marianne anything. She is a detective with Paris Police Prefecture. I suspect she knows quite a bit already. Is that not so, Marianne?"

"Yes, you are right," Marianne replied. "I know most of it already. Please forgive me, Erica. It is late; you must be tired and I have to work in the morning. Perhaps tomorrow we can chat. Are you staying here tonight, James?"

"No," he answered. "I am booked into a hotel."

"Good. We can share a taxi then."

"Yes, OK," he said, just a little reluctantly, I thought.

She put on her jacket, and they left, saying goodnight to everyone. James thanked Henri for his hospitality, saying he hoped Katie and I had a good night's sleep, and he would see us in the morning.

I collapsed onto my bed. I was exhausted. In the other bed, Katie yawned and said she was exhausted. Not that, that would stop her inevitable dissection of the evening.

"What did you think of, Marianne?" she asked.

"She is lovely," I said, refusing to give her ammunition. I knew she was warming up to telling me I should have married James when he asked me to.

Katie mused. "Yes, she is lovely. Can you believe she's a detective? She looks more like a model. She reminds me a bit of a young Catherine Zeta Jones, only with a slimmer face." She paused. "James seemed to like her a lot and she was all over him like a rash. They have obviously been friends, or more than friends, for a long time."

She was irritating me. I snapped, "I thought you were tired." I turned away and pulled the duvet up to my ears.

"I am. I'm going to sleep, right now." She turned away and within minutes she was snoring.

I have always envied Katie's ability to just drop off to sleep. I lay on the bed and stared at the ceiling, for a long time. There was a tight band across my chest, I think you could call it heartache, or maybe it was just jealousy. Whatever you call it. It was making me miserable. Eventually exhaustion overtook me, and I fell asleep.

I awoke in the morning, aching in every muscle. A remnant of the tension of the previous night. There was a light tap at the door. I called, "Come in." It was Henri with a tray, a tea pot and two cups.

It was already nine o'clock before I had a shower and joined Henri in the kitchen. We had finished breakfast before Katie emerged.

Henri made fresh tea, and we sat at the kitchen table. He said, "Erica, Katie, you know I am here to help if you need me."

"Yes, Henri, and we are grateful for your help and for your hospitality," I said.

"You are most welcome. It is my pleasure to have you both here." He hesitated. "James told me a little of your background. I believe he asked your permission first?"

"Yes, he did."

Henri sat back in his chair. "To be truthful I found it an incredible story. I have a lot of questions I would like to ask you, about Lanshoud and about the background behind the story James told me. Do you trust me?"

"James trusts you, that's enough for me. The problem is I wouldn't know where to start."

"The beginning always seems a good place," he said. "Better still, why don't you tell me what you know and I will fill in the blanks?"

"Of course," I said.

"Then it will be as you wish, but let me show you something first, come." Katie and I followed him into the living room. From the front windows, he pointed out a car. "Undercover police," he said. Then, at the back of the building from the bedroom window, he pointed out another unmarked police car.

"I want to be truthful, Erica. This type of protection will soon be taken away and you could be charged for wasting police time."

"Wasting police time?" I gasped. "I was kidnapped by a man in a van. Then I was taken to Langedechu by men impersonating police. Is kidnapping and impersonating a police officer not a crime in France?"

He tried to soothe me with his soft French voice. "Of course it is, but there is no evidence to support your story. I understand how you must feel, but because at this moment there is no evidence that you have any connection to Langedechu, or to the Bernard family who lived there, you may be considered as having trespassed."

"What! They think I was trespassing in my sister's home?"

"Yes, James explained to me that you thought you were related, but you have no proof of that either. Just because you look like Elise Bernard is not enough. I am sorry, but it does not add up. Though you were traumatised when you were taken to the police station, they could not find anything to support your story of having been kidnapped. The police searched the chateau, but there was no evidence of the Germans you spoke of. In fact, there is no evidence that anyone had been living in the Chateau since the Bernards left it, on the day of the rail disaster."

Katie protested, "That is ridiculous."

Henri waited then asked, "Is there anything you can tell me that would support your story?" He was right. I had no proof. I put my head in my hands.

"Erica," Henri said gently. "I want to help you, but I need facts. I know you went before to Langedechu with James. He said he thought there had been someone, possibly squatters there, since the house had been empty for so long."

"I was there too," Katie piped up. Funny the police didn't find anything. When we went with James it was obvious there had been someone there. There were tins of food, lots of beans – they must have liked beans, and things like that,"

"Squatters," Henri nodded. German squatters, were they?" He asked laughing. "Germans who like beans. I am so sorry," he said, unable to stop chuckling.

I didn't like the fact he was amused. "Henri, I am grateful for your help, but I know my story sounds like fantasy and I don't expect anyone to believe me."

Katie added, "If I were not part of this, I wouldn't believe it either."

"Well, I promise you," he said, "I will listen, and attempt to understand what you tell me. James has great respect for you."

"Henri, I know your intentions are good, but equally I know you will not believe me, simply because you won't be able to."

He said, "James will not be back until evening, so start at the beginning. Give me bullet points and, when I need detail, I will ask." He repeated, "just start at the beginning".

I started to speak but Katie cut in with. "I will just sit quietly and listen. Perhaps I will remember things Erica misses out."

"Of course," Henri said.

I knew, there wasn't a hope in hell of Katie sitting quietly. "You should start with the Vansterdams," she said.

"My parents were Wilhelm Vansterdam, a Dutchman, and Mary McLeod, a Scot. They died in a road accident."

Katie added, "A road accident, which was suspicious."

I continued, "A year later I met and married Paul Cameron. I was happy with my life until Paul died in what I was told was a boating accident."

"Only, we don't think that was true; it was very suspicious," Katie said.

"How so?" Henri asked.

I gave Katie a don't interrupt look. "A month after their death I received a letter from a solicitor telling me that it was in my interest to call at his office. I did and when I got there, he told me I had inherited an estate in rural Aberdeenshire and a vast amount of money."

I was about to add that even the solicitor didn't know the benefactor, but of course my pet budgie was in full flow.

Katie added, "That is where she met James who at that time was working undercover as a solicitor."

I started to explain that James arranged to take me to Lanshoud, but I was cut short by Katie.

"That's true, we were there too. Gillian and me. We call her Gill for short. We met him at Stonehaven and from there he took us to Lanshoud. Initially, we were the only three people there, except for Molly the housekeeper and her son-in law, Caleb, the gardener. That was until things started to happen…".

"What kind of things?" Henri asked me. I didn't even get a chance to open my mouth.

"Noises, tapping at windows and doors in the middle of the night, and of course, the horses," Katie said with a dramatic shiver.

Henri exclaimed loudly, "Horses!"

Katie said "Yes, horses. You have no idea. It was terrifying. Phantom riders and figures banging on doors."

Henri looked at me. "Erica?" He waited for me to comment.

"I know how it sounds, but Katie is telling the truth. Lanshoud was a place of ancient mystery that I cannot even begin to explain. It was the resting place of incredible secrets. Mythology surrounded it. Tales that we heard, of riders coming in the night to collect souls were manifested in riders who appeared outside the doors of Lanshoud every night. We were terrified. I..."

"Absolutely petrified," Katie interrupted again. "We called the police, but they wrote us off as hysterical women and put it down to the knocking of old pipes. Only one police officer took us seriously and became a close friend of ours. That was detective sergeant Jonah Seagraves. You would like Jonah – he is a lovely man. In fact..."

Henri, the Master of Diplomacy said gently, "Excuse me, Katie. You are very helpful, but it is important that I hear this from Erica. It is procedure, you see. One witness at a time."

"Of course," she said smiling, totally oblivious to the fact she was being censored, she said, "My lips are sealed."

Henri said. "Please continue, Erica."

Not believing Katie for a moment (Her lips sealed? They would have to be glued!) I continued, "Over the next few months and after a great deal of searching, I learned Wilhelm and Mary were not my parents. They had been put in place as caretaker parents by my real father. I also learned after Paul died that he had been no more than a caretaker husband."

Henri was silent for a moment. Then he asked, "And your real parents, do you know who they were?"

"Yes, but it's a long story. At Lanshoud a young man appeared out of nowhere. He was much younger than me. He called himself Luke Treadstone. He was living and working at CERN in Switzerland. He told me he was my father. Ridiculous as that seemed. He gave a very detailed account of travelling through wormholes from another world, another dimension, and another time. He even claimed to have passed through Hell and was being hunted by demons, seeking to take him back to their master. These, he said, were the riders who were terrorising us. There is so much more to tell you, but I am trying to keep it to bullet points.

"Luke claimed he had first arrived on Earth in Roman occupied Jerusalem. He stopped ageing from the moment he set foot on Earth. He claimed to have been there at the time of the crucifixion and there were artefacts in Lanshoud that backed up his story."

"What kind of artefacts?" he asked.

"Historical religious artefacts."

"From the time of Christ? From the crucifixion?

"Hidden in the cellars."

Henri was stunned into silence. Then he said, "Mon Dieu, what are you saying? That is incredible. If that is true, it is momentous." He took off his specs and cleaned them furiously as though that would help him understand more clearly. "I do not know what to say. The implications of what you are saying are without limit."

"Do you think I don't know that? I am sharing my secret with you, only because James asked me to. You see Henri, I know you have a secret too, that connects to mine. I don't know what your secret is, but it is the only reason I am telling you. James knew you would believe it and help me."

He got up and looked out the window. He stood silent.

Katie shrugged her shoulders, making faces at his back, telling me to speak to him. She almost got caught when he turned and said, "Where are the artefacts now? What happened to Luke? Is he still here on Earth?"

"The artefacts are hidden in safe places in the Vatican and other museums, but Luke is gone. He was enabled to travel back through the Lanshoud wormhole, or gate as he called it, with the help of angels. They closed it behind them."

"Angels? Mon Dieu. You are serious," he said. He shook his head. "This is too much. It is unbelievable."

I said, "It's OK, Henri. It is a lot to take in."

"Forgive me, please, I am overwhelmed by your story. He sat down again. James told me that Lanshoud had been severely damaged and is now being restored. He did not give any detail of how the damaged was caused."

"I am not surprised, because it is probably a stretch too far for anyone's imagination. I am afraid this will be even more difficult to believe."

"Please, continue," he said.

"There was a battle at Lanshoud. A battle you might say was between Heaven and Hell. We were attacked by hordes of creatures that had come through the wormhole. Then we were rescued by beings from another dimension. Beings with names familiar to anyone who has read the Bible or the Torah or any other ancient holy book... angels, Henri. We were rescued by living breathing angels."

I stopped, waiting for his reaction. He stood up, walked over to the drinks cabinet and poured himself a shot of something alcoholic. He held up the glass, to which Katie and I said, "No, thank you." He swallowed the contents in one and sat down again, nursing the glass. He couldn't even look at me. He was speechless and his hands were shaking.

Now I knew he believed me because it took him a minute to pull himself together.

"Please carry-on, Erica. I have good reason to believe you. I will explain but I would like to hear what happened next."

I said, "We survived Lanshoud but, as you know, the building itself was damaged. It would cost thousands to repair. I bought an apartment and an antique shop in Glasgow. With the help of friends, I tried to put my life back together. I enlisted help in the antique business from an expert in that field, a wise and kind, elderly man, called Eli Laskov. He set the business up and, with the help of my friend Gill and her husband Jack, it was soon running smoothly and making a profit. That was when Eli found the ebony box. A box that contained documents, which told of four babies in four countries with an elaborate organisation set up to protect them. It also contained four keys that would close the wormholes in the four houses forever.

"That box changed my life completely. Not only did it tell of my birth but also the existence of my three siblings. Three girls fathered by Luke in test tubes and planted into the wombs of three women.

"Like me with Lanshoud, he set up a bubble around them, great wealth, land, and properties. Caretaker parents and caretaker husbands. The papers in the ebony box gave details of the girls' names, and of the properties gifted to them. I had Lanshoud, Christina had Heiligtum in Germany, Elise had Langedechu in France and Carla had Delcancello in Italy. These houses were built over the entrances to the wormholes.

"Feeling secure, I went in search of my sisters. You know the rest of the story so far. But I suspect James didn't tell you that these wormholes led to Hell, that there were other people like the Die Bruder gang who knew about them. To this day, Henri, there are creatures using them to travel and take souls from our world to theirs.

"There are other worlds out there, Henri, with beings that can see us, that help us or can equally cause us harm. They are travelling back and forth through the wormholes that Luke called gates.

"Christina searched and found me. With help, we closed the gate at Heiligtum. I then came here to find Elise and to close the gate at Langedechu. Do you understand that no matter what stands in my way I must find and close the gates at Langedechu and Delcancello?"

Henri was silent.

I was confused, "I know how this sounds. What I don't understand is why James was so insistent I confide in you. Nor do I understand why, without any proof, you would believe it."

He got up and poured another small amount of alcohol into a glass. This time I saw the bottle – it was Brandy. Katie who had been unusually quiet, whispered, "Is he all right?"

"He took off his specs and rubbed his eyes hard, "Erica, I believe every word you have said, but it is because there is definite proof here in France. However, the detail is better coming from the 'horse's mouth' as you British would say. Tonight, Marianne will explain. She will tell her story."

Chapter Six

The Clairvoyant

We were relaxing in Henri's apartment. Marianne, off duty, after what she said was a horrendously busy day at work, was dressed in a simple white shirt, ankle-length black leggings and black patent stilettos and she still managed to look like a supermodel. There was lots of laughter as there was still some amusing stories she had up her sleeve.

James, of course, was giving her his full attention and she was lapping it up. I found it hard to look at her, she was almost glowing. The truth is she captured everyone's attention; it was impossible not to bask in her magic. I smiled, laughed along with the rest of them but, deep inside, I was torn up with jealousy.

I managed to paste a smile on my face and keep it there, though I could see it had not fooled James or Katie. At one point, I felt I wasn't fooling Henri either, as he interrupted the happy couple by saying, "Enough reminiscing, Marianne, it is time to share what you know of the disappearances with Erica."

She fluttered, "But of course, you must forgive me, please," she said. It has been such a long time since I last saw James."

Katie, forever in my defence (and with a look of innocence that masked her sarcasm) said, "Really! I could have sworn you saw him yesterday."

Marianne didn't miss the fact Katie was having a stab at her. She simply gave Katie a false smile and continued. Turning to me she said, "Erica, James and Henri have told me all about Lanshoud. They told me about your experience of the Wild Hunt. It is without doubt an incredible story but, as it happens, you are not alone. In the last few years, I have had reason to research the history of these horsemen, because there have been many reports her in France and I have read the evidence of sightings held by other police forces in Europe. We have many similar tales here in France, spreading over hundreds of years. Mostly, they have been dismissed as…" she hesitated, turned to Henri, and asked something quickly in French.

"Folklore," Henri replied.

"Folklore," she repeated. "Yes, that is it, folklore. Memories handed down from generation to generation. Tales of villagers disappearing, of dark creatures on huge horses seen and heard thundering down the lanes, and with hell hounds barking at their heels. They were dismissed as no more than that, just folklore. Stories shared by villagers sitting round a fire, sharing a bottle of wine. Tales told to children, to frighten them, ensuring they would return home from playing in the forest before it got dark. That all changed three years ago. That was when two local farm workers failed to return from the fields neighbouring onto the Langedechu Estate. A father and son. Paul and Francois Rousseau. The farmer and his family said they left the farm at the same time they always did. The area was searched for weeks but they were never found.

"The reports of having seen the riders have been, more than once, attached to reports of a missing person. In the fifty-year period between 1970 to 2020, nine people, seven men and two women, went missing in the night. All were in the vicinity of Langedechu. All disappeared without a trace, and no bodies were ever found.

"Only one witness has ever come forward to say he had actually seen the face of the lead rider, which was only two years ago. His name is Edouard Dufour, a local farm worker. Again, there was no evidence, and his story was dismissed as nonsense, mostly because he had consumed most of a bottle of wine while telling his story in the local inn before returning home that night.

"Dufour has been repeating what happened, over and over to anyone who would listen. He claims he hid in the bushes when he heard the horses' hooves thundering in the lane behind him and he insists he saw clearly a figure leading a group of five riders. He swore it was a man, dressed totally in black, and this is where he lost all credibility. He claimed the lead rider had wings and that he saw him fly from his horse directly into an open window in the now abandoned Chateau Langedechu. Of course, to anyone in their right mind it would just sound like a ridiculous lie."

"Would we be able to speak to this man?" I asked.

"Without a doubt, Dufour is a drunk. Offer him a glass of brandy and he will tell all. He will even embellish his story with more lies for your entertainment. In short, he is not a credible witness. I suspect he would be very willing to speak to you, as he has profited from this story many times."

"Have you personally interviewed him?" I asked.

"No, it was not my case, but I have read the files. His story is unbelievable." She sighed, "I think you would be wasting your time speaking to Dufour, but I will arrange it for you if you wish. However, you must be prepared for the fact this man tells outrageous lies."

I interrupted her. "Maybe he does lie, or could it be that his story just seems unbelievable because it makes no sense to anyone who has not seen our even heard of the Wild Hunt? I sympathise with Dufour because my story is equally unbelievable and that is no reason to dismiss it immediately as being lies." I looked to James for support. He said nothing.

"It was not dismissed immediately," Marianne said with a hint of indignation in her voice. "The investigating officer was Hugo Corbin, who is a close friend. It became a passion of his. He was obsessed with stories of the Hunt. He believed there was an element of truth in Dufour's story.

"About a year ago there was a television documentary about the Wild Hunt across Europe. There was a woman interviewed who was considered to be an expert on the subject. Her name is

Adrienne Moreau. Hugo wanted to speak to her. He asked me to go with him. I was reluctant at first. I do not believe in these psychics, but I went, and I was very impressed by her. Adrienne Moreau knew all about Dufour. She believed his story without question, even though she had never met him. She was really quite impressive. I will take you to her if you wish to speak with her. I suspect there are many questions she could answer for you.

I abruptly and sharply said, "No." She was surprised. Shaking my head, I said, "No, thank you. I have good reason to dislike psychics."

"I understand," she said. "James told me about your experience with a clairvoyant at Lanshoud. Emilio Mendez. Adrienne Moreau knew of him. She said he was not what he seemed and was extremely dangerous."

"Well, I can only agree with that" I said. "Emilio Mendez was not human."

I waited for her to laugh or dismiss it as nonsense. Instead, she said, "That is exactly what Adrienne Moreau said."

Henri refilled our glasses and sank down into the sofa beside me. "Erica, given your history, with what has happened here in France, at the chateau, the neighbouring cemetery, the tomb you woke up in, the missing men who kidnapped you, it is safe to assume there may be something there, something not of the natural world, that you may have to deal with when you go back to Langedechu".

"Back to Langedechu! Do you mean I can go back now?"

Henri said, "There is nothing to stop you. I'll put it simply. Right now, you have no credibility with the police, with the exception of myself and Marianne, of course. The police have proved there is no one living in Langedechu and there has been no one living there for many years."

"Then I will go back there as soon as possible."

"Would you like to speak to Madame Moreau first?" Henri asked.

"No, thank you."

Marianne groaned. "You are here to look for these gates, as you call them, is that not so?" she asked. "And is it not so that Katie and James have come to help you search for them?" She looked at James, who suddenly seemed to have lost his tongue. He didn't answer. She turned back to me, "I do not understand. If anyone can help you find them, it will be Adrienne. If anyone can explain why you alone saw the Germans, it will be Adrienne. Fortunately, she is willing to see you tomorrow morning at ten o'clock. You should know you are very honoured, for she does not suffer fools gladly."

"You actually arranged an appointment?!"

"Yes."

"Without consulting me first?"

"There was no point in asking you," James said, "I knew you wouldn't want to go."

Marianne smiled at him, "He said you were a very stubborn woman who didn't know what was good for her." She laughed as she watched for my reaction.

"Thanks for that, Marianne," James said, sharply.

She was baiting me. It was insulting but I chose to ignore it.

There was now a palpable tension in the room. Sitting back, I sipped my wine from the beautiful hand-cut crystal glass Henri had served it in. I said, "Well, James was right. He knew I would be reluctant to be involved with another psychic. I don't care how good she is. I will not go there."

Marianne said, a little loudly, sounding frustrated, "Why not? I will take you there." She threw her hands up. "What is your problem? Why do you have to even think about it? Where else will you get the answers you are looking for? I truly believe that woman can help you. What do you have to lose?"

"Her sanity maybe," Katie piped up. She directed her venom at Marianne. "You have no idea what she went through with another psychic. In fact, what we all did. If you had even the slightest clue you would not be suggesting she go anywhere near this Moreau woman."

"Tell me then. Explain why psychics are so bad." Marianne looked at Katie with wide-eyed innocence. "Because you see, James only told me he was an amazing, world-famous psychic, called Emilio Mendez."

Katie sounded disgusted. She turned on James. "Really James. You just told her he was a world-famous psychic? Why? Were you afraid to upset her? Were you afraid she would think you were either lying or just ridiculous? Why not the truth, that Mendez was a demon from Hell? Why did you mince your words? Were you afraid Marianne will think you are exaggerating or that you were talking a load of crap?"

James' face was a picture. He was visibly annoyed with Katie.

"What is crap?" Marianne asked sweetly looking from one to the other.

Katie smiled sweetly back at her. "It is what comes out of your mouth too dear."

James interrupted, breaking the standoff. "Enough," he said. "Katie, you have no need to defend Erica. She is not being attacked. Marianne is here to help. Adrienne Moreau is a well-respected clairvoyant. I suggest we take her seriously".

"We took Emilio Mendez seriously," I said. "Look where that got us." There was no answer to that, so he let it go.

"I think we should all sleep on it. Don't you agree, James?" Marianne pouted her lips.

"Yes, I do," he answered standing up. "It's late, I think you should sleep on it, Erica, and we can decide what to do in the morning. If you are ready, Marianne, I will walk you to your car." He said to me, "Try and get a good night's sleep. Things will be clearer in the morning."

He gave Katie and I a peck on the cheek. Katie fluttered her eyelashes at him. Sarcasm oozing, she said. "Thank you, James, we so need your good advice."

"James, are you coming?" Marianne called from the door.

Katie smiled at James. "Run along now. You are keeping your mistress waiting." She waved him in the direction of the door.

He stopped. "You aren't by any chance jealous are you, Katie?" he asked her.

"Jealous? Me! In your dreams, James Anderson!" Marianne called him again.

I pulled Katie away before she could say anymore. I said goodnight to him, and Katie mouthed "wimp" to James under her breath. He just laughed at her.

The next Morning, after a general consensus that it was the right thing to do, Katie and I went to see Adrienne Moreau with Marianne, who drove through Paris like a bat out of hell. She took shortcuts down tiny lanes, using her horn to get people out the way or warn them she was coming.

She pushed her way into traffic on the main roads, ignoring the anger of the other drivers she was cutting off. One man threatened to get out of his car but changed his mind when she flashed her police badge against the window. In the back, Katie had turned green by the time we got out. It was the first time in my life I appreciated what it meant to be travel sick.

We were welcomed into the sitting room, in the home of Adrienne Moreau. We were greeted with a warmth that made it obvious that she and Marianne were at least acquaintances, if not actually friends. It was a large apartment in an old gothic styled building with high ceilings and commanding views of the park. It was tastefully furnished in muted lavender and grey colours. It left me thinking that clairvoyance must be a lucrative business.

Adrienne was a widow in her late fifties. She was tall, slim and elegantly dressed in a simple fitted blue dress. She had shining brown hair that was wound into a French roll and held in place with a beautiful filigree gold clasp. She served us with tea in little porcelain cups and home baked cakes. We spent some time going over the details of what happened at Lanshoud, leaving out certain bits that no one in their right mind would believe. She was a good listener, Adrienne, asking only a few questions as Marianne had already provided her with details. She spoke perfect English and explained that she had lived in London, where her husband had a diplomatic post and where she had studied to improve her English.

Adrienne was very professional, and I was beginning to take her seriously, until she asked us to join hands and allow our spirit guides to contact us. I sighed deeply. For all Marianne and Henri sang praises about this woman, it seemed she was no more than a fortune teller. There was nothing else to do but just go along with it. We sat at the table, with joined hands. She closed her eyes and asked us to be silent.

Katie mouthed silently, "Is this a séance?"

I shrugged and mouthed back silently 'I don't know'; after all, the table was devoid of the usual trappings of a fortune teller. No glass ball, no candles, no tarot cards. Just a polished surface. We sat in silence while Adrienne sat opposite with her head bowed and her eyes closed. After a few uncomfortably long minutes, when she finally opened her eyes, they were bleak and unfocused. For some reason, a shiver ran through me, and as though it were contagious, Katie and Marianne shivered too. Adrienne bent her head, but when she lifted it again, her eyes were clear.

"You need to be careful, Erica, something watches you. It does not have your best interests at heart."

Still a little sceptical, I was thinking it was quite a performance she had put on. I asked, "Who is it I need protected from? Is it the spirit of someone I knew who has died. Someone who may have a grudge against me?"

"No, it is not and has never been human. It is an entity."

"What do you mean by 'entity'? Another life form?" I asked.

"No," Adrienne said. These things do not have life in the way you know it. You will not like what I have to tell you, but I will try to explain."

I leaned forward and clasped my hands on the table. "Continue. You can tell me anything. I have seen horrors. I have been terrified to the point of almost losing my mind. Please, tell me what you know."

Adrienne nodded. "The tunnels through time and space, the wormholes, that your father Luke travelled through, are the passageways that these entities have used to enter our world. For centuries they have travelled here. They are not ghosts, as you might describe them, and calling them a life form does not begin to describe these beings. Humans can often sense their presence, but few can actually see them or hear them. These entities, for some reason, have strayed through the wormholes into our plane of existence. Over the centuries, people who have been able to see them have had their body and soul possessed.

"For hundreds of years, mankind has tried to understand them, searched for words to describe them. Christians call them demons. The Islamic world calls them Djinns, which is where the word Genie comes from, but they are nothing like the characters of that name you will find in comic books. The Jewish people call them Dybbuks, and I believe you have experienced the harm they can do, when your friend Jack was possessed."

"Yes, that's true." I said, thinking that when James briefed Henri and Marianne, he didn't leave anything out.

Adrienne continued, "These entities are dangerous and vindictive. They think nothing of invading a human soul, with the intent of causing suffering and misery and ruining lives. For some bizarre reason, if they can be identified, if they can be persuaded to say their name, they can be exorcised – but that is the last resort and often kills the human host. No one has been able to make rational sense of it.

"These entities are eternal; the years of our human life are nothing to them. When thousands of years ago, your father, that brilliant young scientist from another dimension, opened a way through time and space, he unwittingly gave them a means of travel to our world. The entities strayed into those passageways, wormholes, whatever you want to call them, and that enabled them to travel here with ease. Over time, they have wreaked havoc and destroyed many lives. These creatures cannot be destroyed but they can be sent back, if they can be confronted and if they can be called by name. That is when they can be sent back. If you can then close the gates, you can prevent them from ever coming here again. There will never be a need for another exorcism."

I was struck dumb. I didn't think there was anything more I could find out about my father, at least nothing that could shock me. Now I had to absorb the fact he may have been responsible for the destroyed lives, of every demonic possession in history. I felt sick.

"Can you actually see these entities?" Katie asked Adrienne.

"Rarely, but even then, I know they are here."

"How... how can you know? If you can't see them."

Adrienne thought for a moment, she said, "A man born blind must accept that sight exists. A man born profoundly deaf must accept that there is something called sound. To a man who cannot smell, how do you describe the fragrance of a rose? To a man who cannot taste, how do you describe the sweetness of honey? The only way I have to describe it to you is that my sixth sense has elements of all the other senses. For example, I will sometimes smell a strong perfume or a strong foul smell but there is nothing real near me that I can trace the smell as coming from. I can hear voices, but I cannot see anyone and sometimes I see figures that no one else can."

She sat back in her chair. "It is very difficult for anyone to accept the person born with the rare sixth sense. I call it my sense of awareness."

"I believe you," I said. "Katie and I have seen things that are not human. Evil things."

"Not just evil but beautiful too," Katie said.

"Are you referring to angels?" Adrienne asked.

"Are they also entities?" Marianne asked.

Adrienne said, "No, angels – they are a very different species. Servants of the highest power in the existence."

We sat quietly trying to take it all in.

"I want to help you," Adrienne said, "and if you wish, I will go with you, Erica. I will help you find and close the gate at Langedechu."

"Do you know of Edouard Dufour?" I asked Adrienne.

"Yes, I know of him," she said.

"Do you think there is any truth in his story?" I asked her.

"Yes, I believe everything," she said.

That completely surprised me. "Really! You believed him even though he was drunk?" I turned to Marianne, who looked equally surprised.

Marianne said, "Yes? He had been drinking a large amount of alcohol at the time he told his story and has continued to do so since."

"I would do so myself if I had seen what he saw." Adrienne was perfectly serious.

"May I ask why, with such little evidence, you believe Dufour?" Marianne asked.

Adrienne laughed. "A la contraire. May I ask why an experienced detective like yourself, with such overwhelming evidence, chose not to believe him?"

Marianne was as confused as Katie and I.

I asked, "What do you mean 'overwhelming evidence'? There was none. I don't understand... What do you know that we don't?"

Adrienne said, "Think. What was there in Dufour's statement that might have made you decide he was confused, or lying? Take a moment to think, before you answer. After all, there have been, for hundreds of years, all over Europe, many reported sightings of the Wild Hunt. But in Dufour's report there was something very different from any of those and that is why I believe him."

She looked around us with her eyebrows raised, waiting for us to answer.

We sat in silence for a moment, then almost in a whisper, Katie said, "The wings. It was the wings. He said the lead rider had wings."

Adrienne sat back in her chair. "Exactly. The lead rider had wings. Dufour said it flew into the chateau."

Adrienne said, "Katie you have been in Langedechu. What did you see on the wall? Erica, you experienced terror in the in the tomb, but what did you see there? Marianne, translate the word Langedechu."

Marianne took a notebook and pen from her pocket and, in front of us, wrote in large letters, Chateau Langedechu. Then she broke the word down into Langedechu and translated it into, the House of the Fallen Angel. She turned the paper around.

Adrienne nodded. "Now Katie, please describe the painting you saw in the chateau."

"The painting was a white angel standing over and pointing a spear at a dark winged figure, lying on the ground," Katie answered.

"Now you, Erica. The tomb. Describe the statue above the tomb…"

"The statue is the same as the painting. It is a statue of an angel holding a spear over a dark winged angel on the ground." Erica answered.

Marianne said, "I see the connection, Adrienne. You are suggesting that the painting and the statue are a depiction of the creature that Dufour saw, and that the rider he saw fly through the window of the chateau is the same winged creature as in the painting."

"Yes. That is why you should reconsider that man's statement," Adrienne said. "There exists across Europe many witness reports of the Wild Hunt. Not one of them has described any of the riders as having wings.

"Erica, in the story you told of your father, Luke, and the chateau he left to your sister Elise. Do you not see that the painting and the statue in the nearby cemetery may be a warning? Did he leave you anything like that at Lanshoud?"

I had to think for a minute, but straight away Katie said, "Erica, the Harlequins!"

"Harlequins!" Marianne asked. "What are Harlequins?"

I replied, "They are brightly coloured puppets or dolls. They wear a mask and usually have diamond patterned trousers, but they have a sinister history. Many people are afraid of them because they emulate real people, though your glass eyes hold no emotion. They are creepy and their eyes seem to follow you around the room. We found them everywhere at Lanshoud.

"James will give you more detail, but when we did some research, it became obvious that Luke had left them everywhere as a cryptic warning of the existence of the Wild Hunt. The name Harlequin originates from 'Hellequin', from an 11th Century tale of a French monk who was chased by demons on horseback along the Normandy coast. We did a lot of research on Harlequins at Lanshoud, and we found there was enough evidence around the world to make us realise that the danger was real. Now it seems we are being warned again, but this time there is a twist, and the warning lies in the paintings in the chateau and the statue at the tomb."

Chapter Seven

The Butchers Shop

Sitting in the car on the way back, my head was in turmoil. I went over Adrienne's last words to us. "I have told you all I know, and I will give you advice, if you ask, but I will not go to with you to the chateau. I am not as strong as I used to be." She had covered her face for a moment, then said. "I am sorry I cannot do this anymore." Then she had risen from her table and invited us to leave, saying she needed rest.

In the car, halfway back to Henri's apartment, my mobile rang.

It was James. "Where are you? Are you still with the clairvoyant?" He sounded agitated.

"We are in Marianne's car, heading back to Henri's. What is it?" It was his tone, I knew there was something wrong.

"I can't explain just now. Ask Marianne to turn on the radio, the news is on. I'll meet you back at Henri's."

Marianne pulled over onto a side street. On the car radio, the reporter was loud and animated. Marianne translated.

"In the early hours of this morning, at approximately 3am, a six-year-old girl was abducted from an SOS orphan village. The security guard at the village gates was found dead from gunshot wounds and the house mother found unconscious in her bed. She had received a blow to her head and is now in a serious condition in hospital. The other children in the house slept through the night and, in the morning, a 14year old boy, a resident in the house, raised the alarm."

He hesitated, then continued.

"Footage just retrieved from the CCTV at the village gate showed one man shooting the security guard in the head and another carrying the limp body of a child believed to be Amandine Bernard. She is blonde with blue eyes and was wearing pink Paw Patrol pyjamas. The two men were seen putting the child into the boot of a blue Citroen car with a white roof."

The reporter then gave out a telephone number for anyone with information.

"Oh my God!" Katie cried. "That poor wee girl, as if she hasn't been through enough. What will happen now, Marianne?"

"The entire police force will be looking for her," Marian said.

She started the engine again and drove back down the winding street until she found a turning spot and made it back onto the main road. "I must go into work," she said, "but I will contact you at once if there is any news."

She dropped Katie and I off at Henri's and we climbed the four flights of stairs as Katie still refused to use the lift. We had no sooner closed the door than my mobile rang again. It was Gillian.

Gill and Jack knew everything that happened since we left Glasgow because Katie called them, or they called us, every other day, to keep me up to date with the renovations at Lanshoud. Of course we told them about the chateau, my kidnap by Die Brueder and the discovery that Elise had a child. Now Gill said they had heard on the BBC about the child abduction in Paris. "Is it Amandine?" Gill asked.

"Yes, they named her." I told her as much as I knew.

"What next? Honestly, Erica you must be demented. We will soon be there for you. Jack and I are coming over. Jack has rented an apartment in Paris for a month. We were intending to bring Sean, but now I am not sure if that's a good Idea. I will speak to Mum and Dad. I am sure they will be happy to look after him."

"You're right, it's not a clever idea," I said. "But won't Sean miss you?"

She said, "Sean loves his grandma and grandpa, and I am sure they will be delighted to look after him and, at the same time, oversea the work going on at Lanshoud, making sure it is completed in time. My father will be tough on any of the reconstruction workers not working to schedule. I know my father, Erica."

Katie muttered under her breath, "Huh, don't we all."

I nudged Katie to be quiet.

"Is that not a lot to ask of them, Gill?"

Gill said, "Not at all. They are both looking forward to it."

"That's great. When will you be here?" I asked, feeling a sense of Relief.

"I don't know yet. I'll call you as soon as I know anything."

When Gill hung up, Katie said, "Oh her father will manage the workers all right, with any luck they will give him as much as they get. They might even walk out."

I knew what she meant. We both knew him well from our student days, when Gill and Katie and I shared a flat. Gill's father had been an ignorant bully, who gave Gill's mother and Gill and her sister a tough time, but according to Gill he had mellowed with age and was now a doting grandfather.

Katie and I had both been delighted that Jack and Gill were coming. We missed having them around. Though Jack had been through a mental health crisis, a near death experience and what was believed to be exactly the demonic possession that Adrienne described. He had recovered and was back to the old Jack we knew and loved: a university lecturer with vast knowledge at his fingertips. As for Gill, both she and Katie were loyal friends, more like sisters to me, and I could not have managed the last few years without them. They are as different as chalk and cheese. Katie has always been there for me, a friend who has stood by me on so many occasions. A friend who has put her own safety at risk just to help. I do love Katie, but unfortunately, she can be a liability as she frequently has moments when she opens her mouth before she puts her brain into gear. Katie is a daydreamer, who assesses people the moment she sees them, once she has made up her mind there is no changing it. She claims to have an instinct that only she possesses, once Katie decides she doesn't like someone, there is no changing her mind.

Not only in looks but in her demeanour, Katie could pass for someone years younger, but there is also the burden of that childlike innocence. It makes me feel like I have to take care of her. Sometimes it can be exhausting.

On the other hand, Gill is intelligent, quiet, sensible, and reliable. Katie, Gill, and I shared a flat when we were at university. During that time, Gill – who was and still is a beauty – went through more men in those days than I had hot dinners. It continued that way until after she graduated, and she met Jack. I was so looking forward to seeing them both.

James called as soon as I put my mobile down. "I am putting you on loudspeaker," I said, "so that Katie can hear." He told us a woman who couldn't sleep had been out walking her dog around 4.30am. She claimed to have seen a car like the one described in the news. She said a man stepped out of the passenger seat. She described him as tall and heavily built and said he lifted a bundle from the boot of the car and carried it in through the front door of a butcher's shop. He was dressed completely in black.

She thought it might be the butcher carrying in meat, but then thought it was still odd because it looked as though it was covered by a blanket. The driver of the car kept the engine running. She said she felt afraid and that something wasn't right, so she ducked into a doorway and hid there. She said it was only moments later the man came out without the bundle, and they drove off. She went home, got back into bed, woke up at nine and heard the news of the child abduction. Only then did she call the police. The police including Henri are there now.

My mind was running riot and Katie didn't help when she cried out, "A butcher's shop!"

James said, "I'm sorry, Erica. If there is any doubt in your mind that the missing child is Amandine, there is now proof that the bundle carried into the butcher's shop was definitely her. Interestingly, the supervisor of the village told the police that Amandine wore a gold chain with a bright multicoloured, enamelled figure of a harlequin, and that Amandine had worn it day and night since she arrived at the village. The broken chain and the harlequin were found caught on a discarded blanket inside the butcher's shop. There was no sign of the child, or a body, but the forensic team are all over the shop, now that the necklace suggests she was definitely there."

"Was there? Do you mean they didn't find her there?"

"No, I am afraid not," he said.

"Oh my God, James. What have they done to her!" I sat down, my legs feeling weak.

James said. "He might have taken her out the back door. The police are searching all the premises around the shop. Look, they don't know why they took her there. There is no rhyme or reason to it. The man who owns the shop has been a butcher there for thirty-three years. He is seventy years old and a respected member of the community. That doesn't mean he won't be investigated but, as far as Henri knows at the moment, he has no criminal past. The poor guy is devastated and bewildered by the whole incident. Not only him, but the police are also just as bewildered. Look, Erica, I don't think they will harm her. In truth, I think she might be used to blackmail you. Keep in mind she is a valuable asset."

"Blackmail Erica! Who would want to blackmail her?" Katie cried.

I said, "Die Bruder, Katie. They might use her to get the key to the gate at Langedechu."

James added, "It is almost certainly Die Bruder, but it could also be child traffickers. According to information Henri received, there was an incident two years ago when two children were taken from one of these villages by child traffickers. Hence the security guards now. The police did catch them, and the children were rescued. If it is Die Bruder, it is likely they have been searching for her, it is only a matter of time until they will make contact."

"Do you think they know where I am?"

"Not yet, but they will be looking for you, so stay put. Don't go outside. Don't answer the landline in the apartment."

"Where are you?" I asked him.

"I am with Henri. We will both be back soon."

There was nothing to do but sit and wait. Katie turned the radio onto a news channel, but it was in French, spoken too quickly for me to understand. I jumped when my mobile rang; it was Gill. She sighed, "Sean is creating a fuss. He's complaining that it's not fair that we are not taking him to Paris, because he just has to see his aunties. Self- confident as ever, he added that you will be missing him as much as he misses you."

"Well, we do miss him, but will he be OK if you leave him?" Katie asked.

Gill said, "Well, you know what my dad is like. He has sorted it. He knows Sean well. He made him a promise that, if he stayed at Lanshoud and let his Mum and Dad fly to Paris, without creating a fuss, he might consider taking him for riding lessons at the riding school in Aberdeen."

"Brilliant Gill. Tell him if he does well at riding school, I will buy him a pony."

Gill laughed, "He heard you: you're on loudspeaker!"

Sean came on the phone squealing with delight, "Auntie Erica, I love you. Mum, when are Grandma and Grandpa coming?"

"They will be here tonight, and Dad and I will fly to Paris tomorrow morning."

"You will probably miss me, Mum, but I will call you and tell you how I am doing with my riding lessons. I promise I will be so, so, extra good when you are away. Don't worry – you know I will do well. I am an extremely quick learner. Anyway, if you miss me,

I can always get a flight to Paris…" He hesitated. "Oh, there's Dad." Then he ran off to tell Jack about the pony.

I laughed. "He hasn't changed much."

"No, he hasn't," she sighed. "He's growing fast and Jack says his intellect is growing faster. Otto Reinhardt said that by age five everything would slow down, and his alien DNA and rapid growth would slow down too. Well, it hasn't. So far, he has been able to pass himself off as an ordinary child. Did I ever tell you we registered him at the local school?"

"Yes, but it didn't work," you said.

"It was a disaster. He bonds well with other children because he is kind to them, treats them gently as though they were simple minded. He does it in a way an adult would be kind to a child. The head mistress said to put it mildly, racing, football, table tennis, swimming, he very obviously lets them win. He excels at absolutely everything, way above the level of his own age group. Though we have warned him not to correct the teacher in class – he has done so, more than once. His answer is that it is very wrong to fill his classmates' heads with false information. Jack spoke to him at length about it, and he agreed he would tell us, and we would tell the teacher if she got something wrong or left out something that Sean thought was important. That seemed to work well, until the Head Mistress called us in to say to say she thought Sean was a child prodigy and was referring him, with our permission, to the education authorities. Needless to say, that wouldn't work.

"She told us that Sean appeared to have an exceptionally high IQ. They would like to have him evaluated. "Of course, we couldn't do that. Jack said we knew that he was highly intelligent, but we were moving to jobs in Aberdeen to oversee the renovation of a large estate and its conversion into a hotel, and Sean would be sent to a private school there.

"We did register him in an extremely expensive school in Aberdeen and he has learned to rein in his opinions. We knew eventually that we would have to tell him that he was not an ordinary boy. We told him about Otto Reinhardt. He remembered Otto well. We told him about the messenger who said he was a gift to his Mum and Dad. Jack told him the story of Lanshoud. How the angels had helped. We told him that, although he was born to Gill and Jack, he had special DNA like the angels.

"How did he take it?" I asked

Gill laughed. "He knew already and told us we should never worry about him. He could take care of himself. It was so sweet. He said, 'Mum, don't worry. I will look after you and Dad.'"

Gillian and Jack settled into their apartment, which was only walking distance from Henri's, and that evening we all met for dinner. Henri insisted that we eat together at his apartment. He said he loved cooking and wallowed in the praise he got for it. It was tongue-in-cheek, but he deserved the praise. In any other circumstances, it would have been a lovely evening. I would have enjoyed the company, the good food and wine, in beautiful surroundings, in the company of the best friends anyone could have, but it wasn't like that. I couldn't get Amandine out of my head. I imagined the little girl, terrified, or drugged or worse, in the hands of the men seen on the CCTV. I felt sick at the thought of it.

It was obvious to everyone at the table, and they were trying to take my mind off things, but it wasn't working. I pasted a smile on my face, but I had difficulty swallowing as there was an emotional lump in my throat. It was all wrong, us sitting there, eating, drinking, laughing. All I could think of was Amandine. She could be lying somewhere scared, cold, and hungry.

They were all watching me. I could feel their eyes on me, reading my mind. There was an awkwardness in the conversation, in every comment made, as they were so obviously avoiding the subject. They talked about the quality of the food and wine. The décor in Henri's apartment. Gill and Jack's flight over. Argued a little over politics. I tried to join in but there was that lump in my throat that was choking me.

James asked about Sean. Gill and Jack were delighted to talk about their son, how much he had grown, how clever he was, then they launched into funny stories about him. Everyone laughed but me. I could only smile as the six pairs of eyes bore into me. They were avoiding all discussion of the child abduction. I could have bet my last penny that James or Katie had advised them to avoid the topic just for one night.

Jack brought up the subject of Sean's birthday and was proudly telling everyone how he was spoiled by his grandparents. "And his dad," Gill quickly added. Then Jack said, "You know we almost lost him." Katie and James told the story of the nightmare Gill and Jack went through when Sean was a baby, taken from his cot, while they slept. The press were terrible, hinting at neglect and child abuse.

"It was horrendous," Jack said.

Katie added. "It was soul destroying. Gill will confirm how bad it was. I mean, there is nothing worse than a child taken by criminals, or even something worse than criminals. It just doesn't bare thinking about." She looked around. No one spoke, so she continued. "I mean take that poor wee girl, she could be lying in a bed of wet straw somewhere. They could be abusing her, They…" That was as far as she got.

Just then Marianne accidentally spilled a glass of red wine on Katie's pale cream dress. "Oh! I am so sorry, Katie," Marianne said standing up and pushing back her chair. She lifted the saltshaker sitting beside Katie and said if they moved fast, they could get the stain out immediately. Katie started to say that wouldn't work. Marianne and Gill grabbed an arm each and practically lifted a startled Katie to the ladies' room.

Left with the men, it was obvious they were feeling awkward. Jack broke the silence, asking if my French was improving since I had been here. Henri added it was quite good. Jack then switched to Langedechu, asking for details about my escape from my kidnappers. He tried joking about me climbing a tree, but I was in no mood for making light of that experience. I excused myself, saying I would see if I could help.

I went into the bedroom Katie and I shared and found her jeans and a blouse. I walked along to the bathroom door and listened outside.

Gill was saying, "Katie, for God's sake we are trying to keep her mind off it. You are making it worse. Change the subject."

I could hear the girls talking through the door. Katie defending me, as I knew she would. While Marianne filled in the part where apparently James thought I was ridiculous fretting over this child.

Marianne said, "According to James, Erica's behaviour has been appalling. At one point she tried to pass herself off to the police as her dead sister. James told me she is fanatically trying to get custody of Amandine and that is never going to happen, because she has told the police a story of her being kidnapped, of escaping, of possibly killing two people, and she has no proof that she is related."

"Just a minute," Katie said. "Erica is not a liar."

"No, she is not," Gill said, "and I find it incredible that James would make any derogatory remark about her."

"Forgive me," Marianne said. "I was not suggesting she was. I am merely presenting the facts as I was given them. Did you not see how uncomfortable Erica was at the table? Katie, you were upsetting her – did you not feel the tension? I thought she was ready to explode. I had to stop you."

There was a minute of silence then Katie's voice. "Wait a minute did you deliberately chuck that wine over me?"

"Someone had to stop you."

I opened the door before the conversation got ugly. They were all smiles. "Well, did it work?" I asked, holding out the jeans and blouse.

They looked at me blankly. "The wine." I said, pointing to Katie's dress. "Well, I can see it didn't. What a shame."

Katie said not to worry; Marianne is paying for the dry-cleaning bill.

I left them and walked back to the dining room with a smile to say they were just coming. James put his mobile down on the table. "They have found the car – the blue and white Citroen. It was found lying on its side, it had fallen down the bank of the river, near Chateau Langedechu."

Chapter Eight

The Catacombs

I couldn't sleep that night. I tossed and turned most of the time. It didn't help that Katie was snoring like a pig. I got up around six, had a shower, pulled on a top and a pair of jeans, and wandered through to the kitchen. There I found Henri sitting at the table studying a large map that was spread out in front of him. He looked old and tired. He hadn't shaved yet and the grey – almost white – stubble gave his age away. He took off his gold-rimmed specs and rubbed eyes that looked heavy from lack of sleep.

"Good morning," he said. "Did you sleep well?"

"No, not really, but not because your beds aren't comfortable Henri. It's just that…" I hesitated.

"I understand," he said. "I too found it difficult to sleep."

"Has there been any other news yet?" I asked

"No, not yet. Let me make you some tea." He rose to put the kettle on, and I looked over the map. It was a map of Paris. It was old, with faded lines where it had been folded. Outlines of red ink squares and rectangles peppered it and there was one long curved line that looked like a tree branch.

"Is Katie still asleep?" Henri asked. "Will I make some coffee for her?"

"No, she's still asleep. We will be lucky if we see her before nine o'clock."

Henri smiled. "She sleeps like a child then. Katie has that look of innocence about her."

"Yes, that's her exactly, but don't be fooled by her little girl lost look. She has a strong business head on her shoulders. Katie has two very successful gift shops in Glasgow.

"Henri, may I ask about your map? What are these areas marked off in red ink?"

"They are air-raid shelters." He put the tea on the table and a plate of warm croissants. "Please try them, I made them myself, and the raspberry jam I also made. I am boasting, I know, but they are delicious."

I sipped the hot tea.

Henri said, "Please try and eat, or at least taste them. I am, as you British would say, fishing for compliments. I noticed you did not eat much last night, perhaps it is a reflection on my cooking?"

"Really! Now you really are fishing for compliments, you know your food is excellent, so you don't need me to confirm it. Of course, I will have one. Who can't resist the aroma of warm croissants?"

He sat down. "As I said, these red boxes are underground air-aid shelters and this..." he pointed to the long red line. "This leads to an entrance or exit to the catacombs.

"Catacombs! Here in Paris!"

"You are surprised. Do you not know of them?"

"Catacombs! Yes. I mean, I know what they are but the only catacombs I have ever heard of are in Rome."

"You are not alone in that. Most tourists only know of the Roman catacombs, but there are many others across the world, in Poland, in Portugal, in Rabat in the Middle East, in Ukraine in Czech Republic, Serbia and many more. The Paris catacombs are not as old as those in Rome, or some of the others. The Roman catacombs date back to the first century, the catacombs in Paris were not created until the late 18th century. They were originally abandoned quarries that date back to the 15th century. These quarries became the catacombs by order of Louis XV1 when Paris had a major public health problem caused by overcrowded cemeteries and major collapses of the ground under the city."

The first transfers were made from the largest cemetery in Paris, the Saints-Innocents. The remains had to be transferred at night to prevent objections from the public or the churches. These quarries were eventually made into a labyrinth of tunnels and galleries where many famous people were laid to rest, and they are now a great tourist attraction. Thousands of people take the tour every year."

"A tourist attraction – tunnels full of coffins. I don't understand what makes people want to see these things. I have been to Rome many times with no inclination to visit the catacombs there."

"Well," he said, "to begin, with the remains are not in coffins. There are thousands of skeletons or just the loose bones, sitting in piles or sometimes they are formed into decorative shapes, even statues of a sort."

"That's just weird," said the voice at my back. Katie had emerged from the bedroom, pulling on a hoodie over her pyjamas. Henri was right: with her main of tousled black curls, she could easily have passed as a teenager.

"I couldn't help overhearing bits of what you were saying," she said. "Wandering among the dead for entertainment? No, I don't think so, I will pass on that tourist attraction." Henri poured out her coffee and she slumped in the chair beside me, looking at the map. "What is this?" she asked.

"Henri was about to explain it," I said.

"Look here," he said turning the map around pointing to a red square. "This is an air-raid shelter, dating back to the Second World War, or maybe even older, and it lies underground directly behind the butcher's shop seen on the CCTV.

"Do you think that is where they took Amandine?" I asked. "Do you think they put her in that shelter?"

"As I said, the police have searched it. She is not there. Look here. This is an old map I have had for many years. It is a bit faded, but can you see a fine red line here? It a famous entrance to the catacombs. Two old toll houses, named the Barriers d'Enfer – in English they're the Gates of Hell.

"Charming," Kate said, "that would really make me want to visit."

"Yet, they are very popular with thrill seeking tourists. You see here," Henri pointed out another very faint red line. "Here is another single red line that leads from an air-raid shelter to another entrance into the catacombs. I have passed this information on to the special police who deal with the catacombs, because this particular shelter lies behind the butcher's shop."

"Are you saying that is where they took Amandine? No, surely not. The butcher's shop was bad enough but into a cemetery!" I was horrified.

Henri hesitated, then he said, "I am afraid it is possible. Given the finding of the CCTV footage and the Harlequin necklace, they searched the shop and the garden behind it and found the shelter. The butcher knew it was there too, but he had never been down into it. It had been padlocked and the key lost many years ago, so he knew nothing of its connection to the catacombs.

"When the police went to check the shelter, the padlock on the metal doors had been burst open. They went down into the shelter and found it had been used for storage at some point, they found bits and pieces of crockery, chairs and garden tools and some large spiders but nothing to indicate anyone had been there recently. However, there was a threadbare rug on the floor, and when they moved it, they found a round metal hatch. When it opened, they found a ladder going down into the catacombs."

My heart sank. "Are you saying they took her down into the catacombs?"

Katie, elbows on the table, put her face in her hands. "It doesn't bear thinking about."

Henri said. "Look at this map carefully. See how well it was planned. This is a map of air-raid shelters across Paris. He stabbed the map with his finger. "See here, that is the SOS orphan village. At this point, less than a mile away, lies the butcher's shop and it has an underground shelter buried in the garden behind the shop, which has most likely been untouched since the German occupation during the second world war. There is no other explanation than this. I believe the man we saw on CCTV entering the shop handed the child, who will have been drugged, over to whoever was waiting, and they took her through the garden, down the shelter, through the hatch and down into the catacombs.

"We might never have had this trail to follow but for the woman walking her dog, who saw the man enter the shop carrying something. Something that could but may not have been a child. Even then, if she had not heard the news bulletin on the missing child on her radio and called the police we would not be looking here."

Henri continued. "We know from the CCTV that the man left the shop without the bundle he carried in, and he left only minutes after he entered. We therefore have to assume someone was waiting to take the child from him. The CCTV footage is being analysed for everyone who entered the shop earlier that day, but of course they could have come in from the back garden, where there was no camera. Monsieur Costard, the butcher, swears the alarm was set when he locked up the shop. Yet, it wasn't triggered when Amandine was carried in, so whoever was waiting could have taken her down the shelter, then down into the catacombs. Once underground, they would be able to take her almost anywhere in Paris without being seen."

Katie was horrified. "Oh my God, she is not much more than a baby and they took her to a cemetery?"

Henri held his hand up. "Keep in mind the necklace proves she was in the shop, other than that, there is no solid proof that she was taken into the catacombs. The getaway car left the butcher's shop with two men in it and was picked up by other CCTV in the area, but there was no sign of the third man or the child. The special police unit that deals with Catacombs has been deployed there now. They are armed and have tracker dogs. They will have collected a piece of Amandine's clothing from the village to give the dogs a scent to follow."

"Why is there a special unit for the catacombs?"

"It is to find and remove cataphiles."

"Cataphiles! That sounds like an insect or something. Do you have a police unit catching insects?" Henri laughed, and so did I. "What are they then?" Katie asked.

"People who are there illegally," Henri answered

Katie persisted. "As in, you haven't bought a ticket? Are there so many that sneak in that you have to have a special police unit to catch them?"

Now we were all laughing. Henri said, "No Katie. Cataphiles is a term used to describe urban explorers and sometimes just teenagers... The catacombs are a vast network of tunnels, galleries, and crypts. Some passages are extremely dangerous and narrow enough to trap anyone crawling through. Some are flooded with the ground beneath liable to collapse at any moment and that is why it is illegal to go anywhere other than with the escorted tours. Still, they go and take photographs and make videos they then post on YouTube. They cover walls in graffiti and often paint near masterpieces on the walls. They create statues from rubble and human bones. They hold parties, have sleepovers, drink alcohol, and take drugs. The risk is that they get lost in the maze of tunnels. There has been at least one man lost and found dead in the past few years.

"There is also the risk that explorers come across more sinister criminal groups known to carry out rituals, like the Satanists who perform black masses in the caverns. There are rumours of human sacrifice, but no corpse has ever been found.

"Incredibly, in September 2004 the police found a working full-sized cinema in a cavern, with projection screens, electric lights, and sound, three phone lines, and terraces cut out of rocks. In another cavern beside it there were table and chairs and a well-stocked bar. The police could not pin it down to one group as the ceiling was painted with swastikas, Christian, Islamic and other religious symbols. When they returned the next day with more police to dismantle it, everything had gone. Electric cables and phone lines had been cut and a sheet of paper was left that read: Do Not Look for Us."

We sat in silence, Katie and I unable to take in this real-life horror story of the dregs of humanity and the possibility that an innocent child could be exposed to it. "How long will it take to search the catacombs?" Katie asked. "The red line doesn't seem that long. Could we help search? I would volunteer."

"No, that is not possible. Again, as I said, there are too many risks you would be a burden on the professionals. The police and paramedics are highly trained. Often ex-army veterans volunteer, but as far as I am aware, they have not been used. Anyway, that map is not of the catacombs, it is just a map of known air-raid shelters." He smoothed out the map. "This here is a map of the catacombs." He opened another one and spread it out. It looked like a huge, tangled thread. There were hundreds of lines turning and twisting in every direction.

"The catacombs are vast," Henri said. "They are a complex system of tunnels on several floors with over three hundred entrances and over 200km of tunnels and galleries. Because many are extremely dangerous, only a small portion are open to the public, and that is less than 1.5km on guided tours that last only around an hour. If that is where they took Amandine, they could be anywhere in that maze."

Chapter Nine

The Return of the Crone

Around an hour later, Henri took a call from police. It was a report on the jacket I was wrapped in when I woke up in the tomb.

"Stolen! From the police station! You've got to be joking." Katie was laughing. "What? Someone just walked into the station under French police noses and stole a jacket?" She just couldn't stop laughing, whereas I was trying hard not to. It did sound ridiculous, but I was afraid that laughing at French police may have offended Henri.

I said, "I don't understand, Henri. How is that possible?"

Henri said, "I am as surprised as you are, because evidence, items that are related to crime, are securely locked away. In the station these items are placed on shelves within locked cages, and in a locked storeroom. Yet this morning the door lock was found broken and the cage prised apart. That cage is made of steel. Yet no one saw or heard anything. There are four officers manning that station overnight, and there are several CCTV cameras around the building. The thief is not on any of the footage. It is quite unbelievable."

Henri put on his jacket, "I am going down to the station just now. I will call you if I find out anything." He left almost immediately.

Katie and I sat at the table. Thinking aloud, I mused, "What could be so important about that jacket that it would be worth the risk of breaking into a police station?"

Still highly amused, Katie said, "Maybe these local police officers aren't paid well. Maybe one of the cops on night duty was feeling the cold and just couldn't resist a superior quality jacket when one was right under his nose wasting away in a cage. It was pretty cold last night. Maybe he only meant to keep it for the night but nearly got caught and had to hide it."

She was still laughing.

I took a deep breath. "Don't be ridiculous, Katie."

"How is that ridiculous? Have you got a better idea?"

Still in her night clothes, Katie went to get dressed, whilst I paced the floor. I wandered over to the window. Dark clouds hung menacingly over the city that morning, threatening commuters with heavy rain. I watched the Parisiennes come and go, rushing to work, taking children to nurseries and to school. I was thinking how I would have given anything to have the normal life that these people had. I began daydreaming. I was imagining what it would be like if I could adopt Amandine: we'd go shopping together, get her ready in pretty clothes, rush her to nursery or school.

I turned on the TV news channel just as the news reader was speaking about a missing child. He was speaking so fast I couldn't follow his French but, the photograph on the screen was of six-year-old Amandine. I had never seen her as anyone more than the toddler in the photograph at the chateau. No longer a toddler, she was a little girl with long blonde hair, yet I recognised her instantly.

I grabbed the remote control and tried frantically to record it, but I couldn't get it to work. The photo was on the screen for less than a minute anyway, then it changed, showing the house in the orphan village and then the butcher's shop. I tried to follow the reporter, but my French was not good enough and he spoke too quickly for me to pick up any more than a word here and there. The scene then changed to a group of students protesting outside a university. I watched until the end of the news programme then tried other channels, but there was nothing about child abduction on any of them. I went on flicking through channels, not finding anything, I gave up in frustration and wandered back to the window again.

My mobile rang – it was James. I was so glad to hear his voice. He was with Henri at the police station. "Have you found out anything?" I asked.

He said, "No, but speak to Henri."

He passed his mobile to Henri, but he hesitated. "It is all very strange, Erica. Breaking into a police station, it is unbelievable. Stealing a jacket is even stranger. I know this station well. The desk sergeant here is an old friend of mine. The man is devastated. He is near retirement. He will of course be blamed, because it is impossible to get past the desk without being seen. In fact, all four men on duty are now under suspicion."

James put his mobile on loudspeaker.

"What do you think?" I asked him.

He said, "To get past the men on duty and into the locker rooms without being seen or heard, doesn't sound to me like anything even Die Brueder could pull off. I mean it is not physically possible to steal evidence. That room is like Fort Knox. Anyway, a jacket? What could be so special about that jacket? Erica, tell me honestly: do you know anything about where that jacket came from? Is there anything you haven't told us, because this whole thing is bizarre."

"I told you everything I know, you and everyone else, over and over again. I just woke up in the tomb wrapped in it."

"OK. I'll see you later"

"Will you be back for lunch?" I asked him.

"No. I have spoken to Jack. They are on their way over to you. They are bringing you lunch."

I was looking out the window when Katie came back. "I put the kettle on," she said. "Do you want more tea?" When I didn't answer, she repeated the question. "Erica, did you hear me? What are you looking at?"

She came over and stood beside me at the window. When later she told Jack, she said I was looking down at the street below, riveted to the spot. She was right. I couldn't answer her because I was frozen with fear. Katie put her hand on my arm. "Erica, you're trembling. What is it?"

She pulled back the curtains, looking down at the street below. "What are you staring at?"

I had chills running up and down my back and my mouth had gone dry. I grabbed Katie's arm and held on to her, unable to step away from the window. My eyes fastened on the old woman, dressed in black, looking up at me from the pavement across the road.

"It's her, Katie. It's the one I told you about. The old woman from the museum in Glasgow and in the café at Potsdam. That's her, staring at me."

Katie said, "I know, I can see her. It's just an old woman. Why do you think she is staring at you? Maybe she likes the curtains. Well, actually, since we are four stories up, she probably can't even see you, or the curtains, from way down there. She might just be admiring the architecture. It is a beautiful old building." She ran her hand down the velvet fabric of the curtains. "These curtains are pretty cool – they must have cost a fortune. Henri has great taste."

She snapped her fingers in front of my eyes. "Hey, are you listening to me? Why is that woman upsetting you? It might not even be this window she is staring at. She might be cross -eyed or short sighted or something. Get a grip: she is just a poor old woman."

"Katie, she is staring right at me. I can feel her eyes boring into me."

"Well come away from the window then."

She pulled at my arm. I pushed her hand away. "I am telling you. I know it's her."

"How do you know it's the same woman? You can't see her face from here let alone her eyes. Anyway, she looks harmless, like any other old woman."

"Trust me, Katie. She is not like any other old woman. She is evil. Otto told me she is a demon known as the Crone. Her black jacket and long full skirt down to her ankles, the hat with the hat pin – those are the clothes she wears."

Katie sighed heavily. "You do realise you've just described Mary Poppins. Are you serious? Do you really think you can see a hat pin from here?"

Scared as I was, she still made me laugh. Using brute force, she pulled me away from the window and pushed me to sit on the sofa, then she went back to the window.

"There you are. She's gone already. Honestly, you have let your imagination run riot. She may just be homeless, a poor soul, begging from all the businesspeople, office workers passing by. Paris has beggars too, you know. She has probably moved on because someone gave her money."

"No, you are wrong. She wasn't begging. She was just staring up at me, standing right on the edge of the pavement. Not one person passing by has even looked at her. That's how it was in the museum in Glasgow and at the café in Potsdam with Otto. It was as though Otto and me were the only people who could see her."

"Well move, because she's gone now, so I will make you a nice cup of tea…"

Katie never made a nice cup of tea in her life. She was a coffee drinker. Her idea of a nice cup of tea was to threaten the water with a tea bag. Brewing tea was beyond her. I let her push me into the kitchen. I sat at the table looking at the map of the catacombs, while she made tea for me and coffee for herself. We talked about Amandine and how glad we were to have Gill and Jack here in France with us, Jack a powerhouse of knowledge and Gill level-headed and as good a friend as anyone could have.

"They will be here soon," I said. "I will be glad when they get here."

Katie started piling the breakfast dishes in the sink. "You know, I think it's being stuck in here all day that's driving us both nuts," she said in a funny voice that made me look up.

I said, "I know. We need to get out. We can sort something out when Henri comes back." I noticed she was standing focused on the window. She was quiet, too quiet. Katie was never this quiet. She was staring out the window. She didn't answer.

"Katie, what is it?" I got up, I had butterflies in my stomach. I sensed something was wrong, and as I pushed my chair back, it fell to the floor. The sudden noise didn't even startle her. With unblinking eyes, she was staring, mesmerised by something outside.

I knew before I looked what I was going to see. I looked out the window and there she was. I shivered as chills started running up and down my spine. Somehow, the old woman stood level with the window, on a branch of the large tree across the road. There was a strong wind, and the tree's branches swayed but the woman stood still. People and cars rushed by, oblivious to the creature above their heads, standing on the edge of a branch.

I tried to turn Katie away. When I touched her arm, she was icy cold. Frozen like a statue, her knuckles were white as she gripped the edge of the sink. She wouldn't or couldn't move. I tried to turn her head to look at me, but her neck was rigid... then I heard splash on the floor. I looked down there was a pool of urine at her feet.

"Katie!" I was calling to her, but it was falling on deaf ears. I couldn't even shake her; she was frozen solid. With trembling hands, I took my mobile out my pocket and tried to call Gill, but my hands were shaking so much I couldn't push the buttons and the battery was almost dead anyway.

I had to pull down the blind, but I couldn't reach the cord without climbing on to a chair and stepping on edge of the sink. I climbed up and pulled the blind down but, as I stepped back onto the chair, the blind shot back up and there she was – the old woman floated inches from the glass pane. Suspended in mid-air.

She was so close – the familiar face, the hat, the grey hair, the smile, the blood red lips over crooked yellow teeth. The cold black eyes too sat close to the pinched nose, staring right into mine. She was muttering something.

I panicked and fell back off the chair cracking my head on the tiled floor. I almost lost consciousness. I tried to get up, but I was dizzy. I made it back onto my feet just as, to my horror, I saw the window glass melt and two clawed hands push through reaching for Katie.

Horrified, shaking with fear, I tried again to pull Katie away, but I couldn't move her. The phantom hands had almost reached her when. I cried out, "Please God, help us!"

At that exact moment, the doorbell rang. I turned around quickly but then slipped in Katie's urine and fell again. I was trying to get to my feet. The doorbell was ringing loudly, and someone was battering the door. I could hear Gill's voice shouting, "Erica, are you in there?"

I was shaking, but I managed to reach the kitchen door. I was shouting, "Help!" There was a moment's silence and then an almighty bang as the outside door was kicked in.

The kitchen door swung open. I was shaking so violently my legs had given way again. Gill dropped down beside me. She put her arms around me saying, "Oh my God, Erica! What's happened?"

I pushed her away crying. "Katie! Get Katie! Get her away from the window... the woman... the old woman is trying to take her!"

Gill looked up at Katie and cried out with shock, "Jack, get Katie!"

Jack had moved behind me to lift me up. But they both stopped dead in their tracks when they looked up and realised there was someone else standing in the kitchen doorway. Someone had come through the open front door of the apartment.

Jack stood up. The man stepped forward and put a hand on Jack's shoulder saying, "I'll get her."

I passed out at that point

I woke up on a bed with Gill calling my name. I tried to sit up, but she pushed me back down.

"Where am I?" I asked, confused, trying to place the surroundings.

"You are on your bed at Henri's. You banged your head when you fell. We found you on the floor. Don't you remember?"

I rubbed my forehead, then sat bolt upright. "Katie, did you get Katie? Is she all right?"

"Yes, be calm, lie back down. You are a horrible colour. Katie is absolutely fine. It was weird. She seemed to be in a trance at the kitchen window, but she's OK now Otto's sorted her out."

"Otto! Otto Reinhardt?"

"Yes, of course Otto Reinhardt. What other Otto do you know? By the way, he carried you in here like you were a rag doll."

Completely confused, I asked. "How did Otto come to be here? How did he know we were here? How is he even in France? Otto went back to his own world."

"I know. We were as surprised as you are. We didn't hear him coming. He must have climbed the stairs because we didn't hear the lift moving." All we heard was you calling for help, so Jack kicked the door in."

"How long have I been asleep?"

Gill looked at her watch. "About four hours."

"Four hours!" I was stunned. I looked down at my clothes. "Why am I wearing Katie's t-shirt?"

Gill hesitated, then said, "Sorry, I thought it was yours. I had to wash and change you. You were wet and smelling of urine," she said, cringing.

I was horrified. I put my head in my hands. "Oh my God. Do you mean Otto carried me through here and I was stinking of urine? It wasn't even my urine, Gill. It was Katie's." I covered my face with my hands; I was mortified.

Surprised, Gill said, "Katie's urine? I think you are maybe a wee bit confused from that bang on the head."

"No, it was…" I started to explain when there was a quiet knock at the door, it opened, and Katie came in."

"Oh, thank goodness. You look better," Katie said. "You gave us all a real fright," and in the same breath, "Do you know that Otto is here?"

"Yes, Gill said he carried me through here. I was horrified when she told me that."

"Why what's there to be horrified about? He is such a dish," Katie said, dreamily. "I would quite happily have banged my head, if he would pick me up and carry me to a bed."

Gill groaned. "Ignore her. Katie's one-track mind is in full flight."

I said, "I don't understand. You are OK? What happened, Katie? You were frozen in a trance."

"Eh… No," she said, looking perplexed. "You were the one in a trance. You don't remember anything do you?"

"Yes, I remember the old woman. Is she still there?"

"If you mean, 'is she still standing in the street?' No. Don't you remember? I told you she had gone."

"No, I mean in the kitchen, when you were frozen. She melted the glass, and her hands were coming through the kitchen window. I couldn't pull you away."

"There was no one at the kitchen window, Erica." Katie gave Gill a knowing look. She said, "Maybe you should stay lying down for a while. You had a real bang on the head."

There was a chap at the door. "Come in," Gill called. The door opened and Otto came in.

"I see you have recovered," he said.

"Recovered? Yes, thank you. Otto, I thought you had gone, and we would never see you again. How did you find us? Why were you even looking for us?"

He sat on the chair beside the bed. "I am here for two reasons. When you were in the tomb, you cried out for help. It resonated down the wormhole. It was heard and we have a rule where I come from: ask and you shall receive. Seek and you shall find. Knock and it shall be opened to you. I am sure you must have heard that one before. Anyway, you stole my jacket."

I caught my breath. "Your jacket? What do you mean? I don't understand."

"She stole your jacket!" Katie laughed. "It was yours!"

"Yes, she did, and I had to break into the police station to get it back." Otto looked at me raising his eyebrows. "Well? I am waiting. Do you want to explain how it ended up in a police station and I had to commit a crime to get it back?"

"It was yours! Oh, my goodness it was yours! The jacket that I was wrapped in at the tomb."

"Yes, it was mine. I was sent through the portal after you cried out for help. I covered you with it and left you in order to deal with the men chasing you. When I came back, you and my handmade Italian jacket, that incidentally cost me a fortune, and I look pretty good in, were both gone."

"But how did you hear me? How did you find me?" I asked.

"You were in the tomb of the Fallen Angel. That is where the third gate lies, the entrance to the portal, or exit if you happen to come the way I came through. You see, in times of crisis, response is immediate. Just as before, when you need me, I am dispatched."

"But how?"

"No more questions now. I think you should rest, Erica. There are so many things need explained."

"That's a good point," Katie said. "Might I ask, who is going to explain to Henri about his front door?"

Chapter Ten

The Angels are Here

Otto had been talking quietly with Jack. One moment he was there, the next Katie was asking, "Where is Otto?" He had literally vanished, and no one saw him leave. Even Katie, who had been barely able to take her eyes off him, hadn't seen him leave.

Katie asked Jack, "What are we going to do about this door? I am dreading seeing Henri. Can you get it fixed before he comes home?"

Jack sighed. "Don't be ridiculous, Katie, that is not possible. That door is as old as the building, and that is over one hundred years old. The door is made of solid oak – the wood hasn't even splintered. It was just the lock that gave way."

"Well, that's good, surely then it will be easier to fix. Do you want me to find a locksmith?" Katie asked.

Jack sniggered. "You, find a locksmith?" Much as he was fond of Katie, Jack has never had much patience with her. He gave her 'the look', the one he reserves just for her, every time she comes away with something stupid.

Dripping sarcasm, he said, "Yes sure. Here, knock yourself out." He dropped the heavy phone directory onto her lap. "Look up the local B&Q. I will try and believe your French is up to the challenge, Katie."

"Stop it, Jack," Gill snapped at him. "Katie is trying to help. In fact, that's more than you are doing, considering you were the one who kicked the door in, in the first place."

Jack sniggered. He waved his hand in the air. "Oh! I see, of course, it's all my fault, isn't it? I suppose I should have ignored the screams for help?"

Gill shook her head at him and sighed heavily.

He pursed his lips and said, "OK. I'm sorry Katie, but you see, here's the thing. We need a proper locksmith, not just any locksmith, but one who will come and examine the door, then decide if he can repair it. Then he will have to source a suitable lock for that antique door. Antique, do you get it? That's no ordinary lock. He will have to order a replacement, and God knows how long that will take. Still, he handed her the phone book, "Look it up. I hope your French is up to the challenge."

Irritated by the fact he was poking fun at her, Katie said, "You know, the truth is that I find it hard to believe Otto went off like that. I thought he might have repaired the door before he left."

Jack choked on the coffee he just swallowed.

"He has powers, you know," Katie snapped.

Jack groaned. "Powers!" The remark sent Jack off again. "What kind of powers are you referring to? He's not a magician, Katie. I doubt very much he could manufacture a door-lock out of mid-air."

Katie snapped back, poking a finger at him. "You don't know what he is capable of—" she stopped in mid-sentence when the door opened and a rain-soaked James and Henri came in.

"It's coming down in buckets out there," James said, taking off his jacket, shaking off the rain.

Henri followed suit. "Is Otto still here?" he asked.

"No, he's gone," I replied.

"Oh! What a pity," Henri sighed. "Is he coming back tonight?"

I replied. "We don't know, he didn't say, we didn't even know he had gone?"

I had expected Henri to be shocked when he reached his front door, but instead he was remarkably calm. Neither James nor Henri even commented on the wrecked door.

Sensing something in the air, James sighed, "OK, out with it. Why are you looking oddly at each other? What are you hiding? What's happened now?"

"Did you have trouble opening the door?" Katie asked, smiling innocently.

James looked at her suspiciously and in a flat-toned voice, asked her, "Why would we have trouble opening the door? Henri had his key."

"Ah well. Hang on a minute…" Katie got up walked to the door. I followed her. She opened it, it was perfect. The lock was working and the door undamaged. I stood mesmerised.

"What's going on? What are you looking for?" James asked, bemused by Katie, who was now running her hands lovingly over the wood."

"It's a long story," I said.

Henri was an amazing man, with a kind and generous spirit, and he had accepted all the stories we told him over the past few days with no evidence. He even accepted the story of his front door. He sat down, listened, and believed everything, without any hesitation.

I found all of that strange, but in hindsight it was probably because he knew everything about me and my life over the past few years. He was privy to everything strange, weird, and wonderful, which was of course down to his close friendship with James, and his own fascination with anything supernatural or paranormal.

However, this time, it was different. It was all very well for Henri to enjoy the thrilling tales of angels and demons, but the very idea, that the Crone, an ancient entity, something so evil, was not only a living creature, but it had been at his window may just have been a stretch too far for him. I could see he was completely unsettled, though he tried to brush it off, repeatedly saying he was sorry that he had missed seeing the Crone and missed meeting Otto, but then he stood up and with a trembling hand he poured himself a cognac and downed it in one.

Perhaps it was a mistake to have told him about the Crone, but Henri persisted. He had a lifetime of solving puzzles and the detective in him expressed a need for detail. He wanted more, so I recapped the story of the Crone from my first contact, when the demon presented as an old lady needing help in the museum in Glasgow and then again when I was with Otto in the café at Potsdam.

We were sitting in the living room talking over things, trying to make sense of everything that had happened. Henri was a level-headed sensible, no-nonsense man. Yes, he knew my history. I don't know if he even believed any of it, or whether he just had the courtesy not to dismiss it as just fiction and the product of an overactive imagination.

Henri wanted to know why that creature had come to his home and there I was wallowing in misery, knowing in all likelihood I had brought it to his home. He and Jack were researching information online, looking for any narrative they could find about the Crone. But there was nothing.

Two hours later, after extensive research by James, Henri and Jack, there was still no evidence of the existence of a creature known as the Crone.

"Do you think it, that creature, is following you?" Henri asked me.

"I don't know, Henri. It terrifies me to even think about it. Like you, I think I may have drawn it here. Henri, I am so sorry. I..."

Henri said, "Enough, my dear. If you are going to say this is all your fault, I don't want to hear it. That is just nonsense, you are a victim."

At that point, the front door opened. Startled, we all looked up.

"Forgive me. I should have rung the bell," Otto said, "but who is this victim you speak of?"

"Otto!" Oh, my goodness," Katie cried. "We were just talking about you."

"All good, I hope?" he said.

"But of course. How could it be otherwise?" Katie said, beaming at him. "You left so suddenly, without telling us. We were worried about you, and…"

Otto held up his hand. "Stop Katie, I have told you before: there is not, and will never be, a need for you to worry about me." He was a little sharp and that deflated Katie quickly. She was embarrassed. I felt sorry for her, but she never learns.

James stood up. "Henri, may I introduce you to Otto Reinhardt, whom you have heard so much about."

Henri welcomed Otto. They chatted in French so quickly and fluently that I had little hope of understanding. However, I caught one word clearly: Amandine. I stopped them.

I repeated, "Amandine Bernard? Gentlemen, please, what are you saying? You are speaking about the missing girl? Otto, do you have news? Do you know what has happened to her?"

"Yes, Erica, I have a lot to explain. Please everyone sit and I will tell you what I know."

Henri brought a bottle and glasses to the coffee table. He lit the living flame gas fire, and we gathered around on the big soft sofas.

Henri handed Otto a glass. Otto said, "Henri, I think, if that is cognac, your other guests may also benefit from a little glass."

Otto was looking straight into my eye. A shiver ran down my back; I was afraid of what he was going to say. The room was cold, but the fire that sprung to life was now roaring up the chimney. Sitting beside me on the sofa, Gill squeezed my hand, accepting a glass of cognac at the same time. I looked at their faces. Henri, bright and obviously fascinated. Jack and Otto, cold and expressionless. Katie smiling at Otto like a Cheshire cat. James looking at me with a pity in his eyes he couldn't hide.

I took a gulp of the brandy. It burned the back of my throat but, within moments, I felt the effects of the alcohol and started to relax.

Otto said, "I have something very important to tell you and there are things I must explain. First of all, I would like you to tell me what you know about the abduction of Amandine Bernard from the orphan village."

I asked, "Henri, would you explain to Otto please? Tell him what the police already know."

"Of course," Henri said, securing a seat near the fire. He sat back, sipping from his glass. "We have CCTV footage from the gate of the orphan village. We know she was taken at night by two men. She was bundled into a car with another man driving. CCTV from a butcher's shop in the area showed the same car pulling up outside and a man carrying a bundle from the car into the shop. We believe the bundle was the child, whom they had most likely sedated. The man left only minutes later, empty handed, leaving us to assume that she had been left in the shop. He entered the waiting car, and they drove away. Unfortunately, the footage was not clear enough to allow us to identify him, or the driver, or the registration plates."

"How then can you then be sure it was Amandine?" Katie asked.

Henri replied, "Because when the shop was searched, there was a necklace found. It was confirmed by the matron at the orphan village to be the one worn by Amandine."

Then Henri continued. "The man who carried her, was in the shop for no more than five minutes. We therefore assume there was someone waiting to take the child from him. We think there were three men involved. The car driver, the one who carried the child, and the man or woman waiting in the shop.

"Our forensic team later discovered a bomb shelter in the garden with a ladder leading down into the catacombs. There is sign of disturbance and we believe the child was taken that way."

"That's horrendous," I said, my skin crawling at the thought of that little girl in the catacombs, the home of the dead. It was just too awful to contemplate.

Henri said, "Since there was no further sign of Amandine, in the shop nor on the CCTV at the front of the shop, we have to assume she was taken by this third person through the catacombs. If he knew his way through, he could take her anywhere in the city unseen.

"The car itself was found a few days later. According to the witnesses, who were a man and his wife out walking their dogs, they claimed to have seen two men walking with a little girl towards Langedechu.

"Although the child seemed happy, they were concerned by the rough, unkempt look of the young men who kept her between them, swinging her in the air. The couple, Robert and Petra Bouchard, had seen the reports on television of the missing child from the orphan village and this little girl fitted the description given on the news channels, so they hid and called the police.

"The police officer they spoke to warned them that following the two men could be dangerous and advised them to stay out of sight and he would send a car. They did as he advised.

"The Bouchard's described the men as being young, both very tall and with broad shoulders. They were wearing long leather coats, almost to their ankles, and leather boots up to their knees. They both had long curling hair, one with light hair, the other dark. Furthermore, the wife said that, when their coats flapped back, she could see they were armed. She said the child seemed happy with the two young men and laughed as they swung her between them, as they walked the path to the chateau. The police have since scoured every inch of the chateau, but there was no one there."

Very tall young men? Long hair? Long leather coats? My mind was working overtime. Could it be the same men who rescued us at Lanshoud? As though he could read my mind, Otto said, "Yes, Erica, I believe it was them."

Henri picked up on it instantly, "What! you believe it was them? What are you saying? Do you know these men?"

"Maybe," I said.

"Mon Dieu!" Henri was stunned. He turned to me. "And you have said nothing till now? You may know of possible suspects, but you say nothing!"

"I am only guessing, Henri. It was Otto who suggested we may know them." I said this looking to Otto to comment again, but he didn't.

Otto was strangely quiet. Then he said, "I believe you have a photo that might jog our memory, Henri."

"Yes, I do." He took it from his wallet and handed it to me.

"What is going on here," Henri asked. "Bizarrely, when I told James about this almost blank photo, he said immediately that you or Otto might be able to explain. The fact is that the woman, Petra Bouchard, hid but took a photo on her mobile phone. I have a copy of that photograph here. You will want to see it."

He handed it to Jack who sat beside him.

Jack peered at the photo closely. "What is this?"

Henri said, "Pass it around, Jack. I think you will all want to see this." It is the photo taken of the two men and the child. It was processed by the police laboratory. No one can explain why the image of a laughing child swinging in mid-air is so clear. She is not holding onto anything, yet her hands are positioned as though she is being supported by something or someone... even though there is no one else there."

"What does that mean?" I asked. "Is it a fault in the mobile's camera?"

"There is no fault in the woman's mobile," Henri said, defensively. "Our forensic teams do not make mistakes."

"He is telling the truth," Otto said. "Those two men cannot be photographed. Their image cannot be captured by any camera."

"Mon Dieu! What is this? A moment please," Henri said. "Otto, are you saying you know these men?"

James was sitting with his hands on his knees, looking into the glass of cognac. He said, "I think Henri, apart from you, we can all guess who they are."

Gill put her hand on my arm. I said, "I am fine, Gill." Although I wasn't.

James asked, "Otto, what do you know? Please tell us."

"Yes, please tell us all," Henri said, obviously annoyed. He was not entirely happy with Otto's revelation that he had information which had never been given to the police. "Who are these men?" he asked angrily.

There was silence as Otto hesitated, choosing his words carefully. "Forgive me, Henri. They are not men."

Henri screwed up his face, he was taken aback. "Not men? What are you saying... not men?"

Otto drained his glass and Henri quickly refilled it.

Otto said, "Look, Henri, there is no point in you pretending that you are not aware of my background, who I am, or even what I am. I know that James has explained it all to you. As for the two men, Rafael and Uriel, they are of my kind, but they are more powerful than I am, and they can be very dangerous. They are warriors, they are soldiers of our master. They have most likely been sent to protect Amandine and her mother and, more importantly, to destroy the Crone!"

I gasped. "Wait! Wait, wait a moment. What did you just say there? What do you mean her mother? Say that again."

"How else can I say it?" Otto said. "They will have taken the child to her mother, who is in the Chateau."

I was absolutely stunned. "Her mother? Elise? My sister? She's alive?" I was stunned. My heart was thudding in my chest. "Oh my God, Otto, are you saying Elise is alive?"

"Yes Erica, your sister, Elise Bernard, who was known as Elise du Sante, is alive and with her daughter Amandine somewhere at Chateau Langedechu. Though her husband died in the train crash, she did not die then. Furthermore, Amandine was never at an orphanage. It was all staged to make it look as though she had been kidnapped from one. All set up by Die Bruder."

"I can't believe it. Where has she been all this time, Otto? Where is Elise now?"

Otto sighed. "She has been held prisoner, at Langedechu, since she was found by Die Bruder. They kept her, intending to blackmail you. They know you have the keys, Erica. Think about it. Those keys are the most powerful tools of time and space. Die Bruder and the Crone will stop at nothing till they get them."

I felt sick. "Then she was here, when I was here, and I didn't even sense it. I ran away. Otto. I ran away from the chateau and the child."

"Sit down," James said, pushing me into a chair while he tried to refill my glass. "You couldn't have done anything anyway."

I pushed the glass away. "No, thank you, no more. I am alright. Otto, tell me please. Tell me what you know, why did she go to Langedechu?" "Elise didn't go there. She was taken there. Die Bruder were searching for her, and by chance, they found her at the railway crash site. They took Elise and Amandine to Langedechu, where Die Bruder have been hunting for the third gate. They knew it would be somewhere in or near the chateau. Their intention would have been to hold Elise, and her child, here as hostages. They would then blackmail you into handing over the key to the gate of the wormhole at Langedechu, but their plan failed. I don't need to tell you what I think you already know; they practice what we call black magic."

Otto said, "They seek power, Erica. You know this already. I have told you over and over. It is all about power, and they believe they will find it through control of the wormholes, that would give them access to other worlds. They summoned the Crone. She came from another dimension. She came through an open wormhole, probably the one at Lanshoud, and she has been following you Erica ever since.

"She seeks not just children, but the keys to all the gates that would allow her to change worlds and collect children, as many as she wanted. Die Bruder's intention all along was to sacrifice Amandine to her and, in return, the Crone would lead them to the gate, but their plan failed and, by the time they traced Amandine to the orphanage, someone had taken her. I put my hands in my head."

James sat beside me. "I want to go to the chateau, now," I said.

"No, not now," James replied. "It gets dark quickly. It would be better to go in the morning. We will take you there. Henri and I will go with you."

I couldn't wait. While tea was served, I sneaked out supposedly to the toilet. They were all talking so it took them a minute or two to realise I hadn't come back.

I didn't want to wait, I wanted to go then, right that minute. They heard me close a door and they came running; they all tried but they couldn't stop me.

I ran downstairs, knowing James and Henri would follow me through the winding streets. I hailed a taxi the minute I reached the street, and I managed to persuade the driver, by promising to pay double his fare if he could take me to Langedechu.

Just as he started his engine and was about to drive off, the door of the taxi opened, and Katie jumped in.

"What are you doing?" I cried.

"Don't start, Erica. You know I won't let you go there alone."

"I wasn't going alone. As you well know," I said. "James and Otto are going with me. They have a cab waiting."

"Eh yes, I noticed that," Katie said. "I asked them to wait for us as we were going to the market first. They weren't too happy about that, but I said you wouldn't mind."

"What? Katie you better be joking."

"No, I'm not. Really Erica, you worry too much. It is all sorted. I have persuaded the taxi driver to drop us off at the market," she said. Did you see those stalls? Oh! Did you see that gorgeous pale green dress? Did you see it? It would look great on me; green is my colour. C'mon Erica, have you never noticed my skin has a translucent glow when I am around anything green?"

When I didn't spend the next few minutes agreeing with her and her love of green dresses, she went in a mood, typical of Katie.

"Look, Erica," she said, "just drop me off here at that shop with the green dress in the window. I can try on a few, then you or just the driver can pick me up on the way back..."

"Absolutely not, no Katie, you got yourself into this, so just stay in the cab till we get there, or you can go to the chateau with James and Henri."

"No, I can't. They wouldn't let me in their car. Even though I told them where you were going."

"What!" I cried. "You told them where I was going?" I could have strangled her. "OK you can come with me..."

The driver sped through the traffic. I had no doubt James and Henri would be annoyed with my uninvited passenger, Katie. In fact, they would soon be chasing us.

The taxi driver, whose English was perfect, suggested he take a route that would be difficult for anyone who was trying to follow me. I agreed. At first, he first crawled down streets until he reached Rue Saint Dominique, then he switched to Avenue de la Motte-Picquet in the 7th area, famous as one of the best market streets in the city. There he was sure they would lose James and Henri, who by this time, he knew were following us.

Along this cobblestone road, were authentic cafés, boulangeries, and countless specialty shops. The traffic and the pedestrians were horrendous. It's where Parisians go to pick up all sorts of local groceries and think nothing of stepping off pavements in front of taxis. My taxi driver was amazing.

He hung out his window, yelling abuse at people who just leapt out in front of him.

James and Henri did not fare so well; James was left trying to convince a lady that he had not tried to kill her when he had slammed on his brakes and missed her by inches.

Chapter Eleven

The Fallen Angel

The taxi dropped Katie and I off at the entrance to the chateau, but the driver could not get away quick enough. I think he was anxious and spooked by the silence, and the mist that was growing darker by the second. He had been trying to tell me something. I knew he spoke English, but he was rattling away in French so fast that I could only recognise a few words. Still, I managed just enough to realise something had scared him and he was not going to wait around until James came.

There had been a strong wind blowing and black clouds peppered with the threat of rain in Paris, but at the Chateau, there was no wind and no rain and no sign of life. There was a thick mist growing and it was deadly silent. We thought it best to make our way to the steps and up to the door, listening, watching for any movement, but there was none.

It was so eerily quiet that I shivered. I had made a mistake coming here alone with Katie. In fact, it was always a mistake to go anywhere creepy with Katie; she would always panic.

The driver took out and lit a cigarette. "Is he just going to sit there?" Katie asked. "Could you not persuade that lazy git to shift his butt for a few minutes and walk us up to the chateau door, because that mist is getting thicker and I think I saw something moving, something ghostly out there."

I was about to say don't be ridiculous Katie, we can just go up ourselves, when I saw what Katie saw. In the deepening white mist, you could just about see something tall and thin and black that looked like it might be a man.

I asked the driver to come into the chateau with us, or at least wait until my friends arrived. Annoyed, he refused blankly. Swinging his hands in the air out the window of the taxi he cried, "No, no, no. I leave now." He revved the engine even as I begged him to stay. I offered to triple his fare, but he would have none of it. He was in so much of a hurry that he was about to leave without any fare at all.

The taxi's engine was purring. I asked him what he was afraid of. He took offence at that, denying that he was afraid of anything. He then slammed and locked all the doors in the taxi.

The taxi started to move, crawling very slowly. The driver rolled down his window and stuck his head out, looking back at Katie and me as we stood shivering. He shouted, "You are madwomen to stay here and, if you have any sense, you will get in and come back with me now!"

He quickly rolled up the windows again.

Katie tried pulling the door and then she kicked it. "And how are we supposed to do that, idiot? You have just locked all the bloody doors."

"Katie, stop," I whispered, "You are making it worse. The driver knows already we are waiting for someone. He is not going to hang around while that mist is growing stronger, and anyway he thinks he has seen something out there."

"Well, that's no surprise. I know his kind," she said. "He is a selfish rat. He is just after our money!" she slapped the window again and shouted at him. "Did you hear me driver? You are a selfish rat!"

I said, "Katie, stop it."

"Why should I?" she said. "He doesn't care that it's getting dark, and there is a mist crawling, winding its way towards us. He doesn't care if we get murdered." I had to grab her coat and pull her away as she battered the taxi window.

The angry driver opened his window just enough to swear loudly at Katie, his English was perfect for that. I stepped between Katie and the driver, who was now hanging out his window. I reminded him again not to worry as we had friends who would soon be there.

"Friends? Oh, is that right?" the driver said, sarcastically. "Are your friends going to deal with the creature that you think is hanging around here in that mist and what about the mad woman?" he asked, pointing to Katie.

"She is not a mad woman," I said angrily.

"Oh well that is very good to know," he said, smirking. I so wanted to punch him.

He said he was just a little reluctant to leave us, but in truth it was obvious that fear had overtaken him. He couldn't move quickly enough, and so he drove off, leaving us standing in the moonlight, in a creeping mist with a wind getting stronger and howling. I knew it; I had a feeling all along that he was never going to stay with us. In the end, he took off, driving like a madman, leaving us standing at the bottom of the stairs, staring up at the huge chateau. So anxious was he to get away that, to Katie's delight, he forgot to collect his fare.

The taxi moved away. There was no other sign of life. Then the rain and wind died down, but it was still bitterly cold. My heart almost stopped when suddenly I saw what looked like a ghostly figure. It was black with what seemed to be black wings, floating in a white mist.

I would not be exaggerating if I said Katie and I were terrified. The figure was floating slowly towards us as we panicked. Katie cried "run" at the top of her voice. She grabbed my arm, and we ran up the stairs to the front doors of the chateau. It was deadly quiet, and I feared the doors would be locked. However, they opened easily. Maybe it was a miracle that brought angels to our side that night.

With an eye on the floating shape and holding on to each other, Katie and I ran towards the stairs. We climbed them and it took every bit of courage for us both to push the heavy doors and slip inside.

"Dear God," I pleaded aloud, "please don't let me go through that again!" Katie had been clinging onto my arm, holding me up when I hesitated. When I touched the brass knob, the oddly shaped lion's head on the wooden door, it screeched as it swung open wide, and so we stepped through into the hall of Langedechu and pushed the big doors shut behind us.

My fear was growing fast. It was bitterly cold. I had shivered when I stepped inside, and it all came back to me. There was no light. It was just a huge hall with marble floors and stairs with marble steps and paintings all covered with cloth. Memories of when I had been kept as a prisoner by the Die Bruder gang, and when I had escaped and woke up in a sepulchre hit me hard.

Standing in the hall, shaking with cold, we were clinging to each other and trembling. There was no latch or key on the door. We hadn't even looked to see if that ghostly black thing was still out there, in the mist, because Katie and I were too scared to look for it. I just managed to pull myself together and begged my guardian angel again to help me to find my sister and her child.

Just then there was a flash of light outside and the sound of a car's engine. Katie ran to the sitting room window, where she could see from the huge bay window the lights of the car coming up the driveway.

Praying that it was Otto and James, we hid behind the big velvet drapes at the window. The mist was still thickening, and we could barely see the shapes of a driver and another man as they left the car with the car headlights on. They were running quickly to the stairs.

Katie looked out the window and thought she could see the strange shapes in the mist again, and that panicked me too, so I hid behind the big sofa. We heard the screeching of the big doors at the entrance and heavy footsteps in the hall. The sitting room door was lying open and the footsteps from there were getting closer. Then a familiar voice called out, "Erica, Katie, come out, we are here."

I knew that voice, so I stood up. "James, is that you?" I cried. "Yes, it's me and Otto is here too," he shouted back. I threw myself at him so fast I knocked him over onto the sofa. I was so relieved. "I am so glad you came, James."

"We told them what we saw and thought they would be relieved. Instead, one very angry James said, "Why did you not wait for us? You know, Erica, sometimes I think you have a death wish." He was really angry, like I had never seen him before. He carried on, "Katie, you are just as bad and just as stupid. You knew Erica was a prisoner here at one point. You know what happened to her here. Then, just as though it was a little adventure, the two of you came here alone."

He turned to Otto. "Those two need their heads looked at," he said before stomping off.

"Did you see the figures outside in the mist?" I asked Otto.

"Yes, we know what they are," Otto said. "James is right. You have been very foolish to come here, especially when it is dark. Ten minutes more and she could have taken you."

"She? Who do you mean?" I asked. "Who would have taken us?"

"Oh, waken up, Erica. The Crone!" James said. "You have crossed her path her before, at least twice. She is a demon of the worst kind, Erica. She has followed you already and she will continue to follow you until she gets the keys, and she will kill anyone in her way!"

Otto said, "It's even worse now, Erica; even the Crone will avoid this place, yet she still aims to rule every planet in the universe. She needs those keys for that, and she knows you have them."

Otto asked Katie, "What did you see in the mist?"

Katie said, "It was all white with a sort of grey, then a black figure with wings appeared. It was fuzzy. I couldn't see it well because the mist kept coming and then receding as though it was dancing."

Otto said, "Stay together because I know what that thing in the mist is, and it is very dangerous."

James said, "Look Erica, we are going to check out the rooms. You and Katie stay close to Otto, because the Crone has no power over him, but she can rip you or Katie, or me, to bits."

We waited and waited until Otto and James searched every room, but there was no sign of anyone else. It was eerily quiet.

James wanted to speak to me, but I was in no mood for a lecture. There was nothing I could say that would appease his anger at me for taking off to the chateau without telling anyone. He called me everything: a stupid idiot, a fool, a headcase etc, etc. He even asked me if I had a working brain in my head. He added, "Henri and I will search the rooms. It will take about ten minutes. Don't turn off your mobile."

"Why do you think I would I do that?" I asked. "I am not that stupid. Anyway, my battery has less than a minute of charge."

"No surprise there then," he grunted. That went down well; he knew I frequently ran out of battery.

I was angry – no, furious would be a better way to describe how I felt about the selfish taxi driver, who had left Katie and I standing there in the driveway – but I was less angry than James who could not find enough words to describe what he called my stupidity at not making sure my mobile was fully charged. Not that it seemed to matter to him that I was scared and angry and shivering with the cold.

There was a strong wind building up and the trees were swaying and making a howling sound. We stood just inside the large doors that had been left slightly open. "Ten minutes" James had said, and he and Henri would never let me down. He would almost be there by now. True to his word, ten minutes later, James came running up the steps, two at a time, and into the hall with Otto and Henri.

At the same moment, a child cried out. We turned. My heart skipped a beat. A child sat on stairs in the hallway, a little girl, with long blonde hair. She was nursing a doll and singing a little French nursery rhyme. She glanced over and, as though she couldn't see us, without even blinking, she just carried on singing.

"Go to her," Otto whispered to me.

"No," I said, "she is less likely to be afraid of you."

Even so, I moved slowly to join the little girl sitting on the stairs. My heart was racing. I said my name was Erica and asked for her name in return. She didn't answer and just looked away. I held my breath; she looked so familiar, like my sister when she was that age. A chill ran down my back. I wondered if we had really found my sister's child...

At first the girl was nursing her doll as though we were not there. Then she started singing softly to the doll. She ignored me completely when I started singing the little song with her. I told her I had learned the song from my own mother when I was a little girl.

My singing had no effect on Amandine; she simply turned away from me, bending over, covering her eyes with the hem of her dress.

Otto, who was of course fluent in all languages known to man, sat down beside us on the stairs. At first, Amandine turned away, ignoring him too. He told her not to be afraid. She pointed again to the door in the wall just opposite the stairs, and in perfect English she said, "Mummy is in there, the men put her in there. They said, if she tried to run away, the black creature with wings in the painting would kill her. I saw the painting," she said. "The black man with horns on his head. He had wings too, and in the painting he can speak."

As she burst into tears, that last comment sent a chill creeping up my spine. I put my arms around her trying to comfort her, but she kept saying "Mummy" over and over and pointing to the door.

I asked the little girl, "What's your name?"

She said, "Mandy. Daddy called me Mandy, but my name is Amandine. The train killed Daddy. He is in heaven now."

Now I knew for sure, this was the child we were seeking.

Tearfully, the girl said, "Maybe Mummy will come back."

My heart skipped a beat.

This little girl may be my niece, my sister's child, and she doesn't even know me or even recognise my name. As though we were not there, Amandine continued singing her little song, losing the words through the tears that were now running down her cheeks.

I put my arm around her. I asked her again, "Mandy, can you take us to Mummy?"

She looked up at my face and screamed, "I told you! I told you and nobody listens to me. Mummy is in there." She pointed to the door again.

I said, "We are listening to you, darling."

Weirdly, she said with a soft voice, "Do you know you look like my Mummy?"

"I suppose I do, Amandine. Afterall your Mummy is my sister."

Suddenly, Amandine leaned over and pointed to the door opposite again, saying, "Well, Mummy is in there. If you are her sister, get her out. Can you get her out?" Once again, her whole face was changing into anger.

James, who had been listening to the conversation, walked straight to the locked door, then he turned back to the girl. He asked her if she was sure her Mummy was in there.

She cried out, "Yes, yes, I told you to stop asking me. She is in there." She stamped her foot. She was frustrated now and kicking at the door.

Of course, the door was made of solid cedar wood and firmly locked. James knocked, but there was no response. He tried kicking the door and calling, "Elise". He raised his voice louder and louder, but to no avail. Otto signalled to Amandine and put his finger to his lips.

To this day I never understood why Otto, who had such supernatural power, didn't just open that door. I was beginning to doubt if he was what we thought he was; if he was what James told us he was, he should never have needed a key to open any door.

I spoke gently to the young asking her again whether there a key for the door where Mummy was. Amandine spoke simple French and English, and she was asking Otto to take us to where her mother was. She began crying, again getting more, becoming more upset.

Sitting between Katie and me on the stairs, in the hall, the girl reached out to Otto and, to his surprise, she slipped her little hand into his and pulled him to follow her. I followed him too, but he was signalling to me to stay back, leaving me confused as to why she was taking him there. Afterall, those stairs ended in an empty cell.

Otto asked the child again, "Amandine where is Mummy?" This time the girl turned on Otto, and she was furiously angry, the tears streaming down her face. "I told you: Daddy is in heaven, but Mummy is there."

Crying out for her mother, she ran to the locked door, trying to push it, hitting it with her little fists even though she was hurting herself.

Realising what she was doing, Otto turned her gently by her shoulders and pointed to her to go back and sit again with me on the stairs. The girl refused to move at first but then she sank to the floor crying.

Otto put his finger to his lips, signalling quietly to me to stay sitting beside her again on the stairs.

James asked Otto, "Where did Amandine get the key in the first place?"

Otto said, "She has had it all along. She has kept it under her dress. We just didn't realise she had it until now."

"Otto, she is desperate to see her mother," I said, "and we don't even know what's behind that door. Where can we get a key?"

James tried to take the key from Amandine, but she wouldn't let it go at first. He asked her again if she knew what was in the room. "Just Mummy," she said. "I told you again and again: they put Mummy in there, and I was with her when they took her away."

"Who took her away, Mandy? I asked. "Is Mummy still in there?

"No," she said, "I told you. They took her!"

"Who took her?" I asked.

"The black thing," she said, breaking down into tears. "

I looked at James. He shrugged his shoulders. "Just go with her," he said quietly. "She doesn't know what she's talking about."

I put my hand out. "You have a key, Amandine. Can I have it please?"

Amandine hesitated then pulled the key from the pocket on the inside of her apron. Then she let James take the key from her so we could open the door of the empty room. It was nothing but bare walls, not even a bench. As soon as the door began to open, Amandine shot passed me and managed to get into the room, crying "Mummy!" But of course, Elise wasn't there. It was no more than an empty prison cell.

Amandine was distraught, now crying loudly. "Where is Mummy? Where has she gone? She was in that room. I think the monster took her!"

"What monster took her?" I asked, where is it?"

"What did it look like?" James asked, softly.

She snuggled into James and said, "It's black. It looks just like the monster in the painting."

Gently James asked her, "What painting, Amandine? Can you show us the painting?"

"Yes," she said, "I'll show you."

Taking my hand, holding it tight as she could, Amandine pulled me towards double doors that lay open along the passage. She said, "Mummy told me to never go in that room because the monster would steal me away through the painting and so I am not going in that room ever again. But, if you just open the door a little, you can see it on the wall."

"See what?" I asked.

"A painting of it. It has big black wings and a big tail with scales like a dragon, and it has big red eyes and big black teeth. It's a monster. It frightens me."

Katie laughed and groaned. "Honestly Amandine you need to be a good girl and not make up stories like that. You will frighten us all."

"Katie," I whispered sharply, "that's not funny. Get a grip – the child is telling the truth, as she knows it."

Amandine now had tears running down her cheeks and she threw herself at me saying, "I saw it, Erica. I did see it. The doors were opened, and I saw the bad thing in the painting. I didn't know what it was, but it was scary." She looked at our faces. "You don't believe me, do you?" she cried. "No one believes me – only Mummy. She said that it was walking in the house."

"I believe you," I said. "Who doesn't believe you, darling?"

"Everyone, except Mummy," she said. "Mummy knew what it was. It wasn't just a picture. I heard Otto tell Mummy it was real, and he said he would stay but we had to leave the chateau."

Elise said, "Katie, I know you would rather stay here with Otto, but we must leave."

We followed Otto to the large open sitting room at the rear of the chateau. There at last stood James and Henri in the doorway.

My heart stopped a beat when Amandine tugged at my sleeve, pointed, she squealed, "Look! It's Mummy."

Pale and exhausted, held together by James, who was half carrying her as she stood beside the large fireplace, was a woman. She was pale and her eyes were swollen from crying; she was a worn-out shadow of my sister Elise. When she saw me, Elise dropped to her knees and Amandine ran to her, almost knocking her over. Amandine clung to her mother, her mother hugging her in return. I threw my arms around them both and we cried tears of joy that Elise was here and alive.

Otto said, "Now we have to go. James and Henri will take you to the car.

As we walked back to the other side of the house, we passed the open double doors of a larger sitting room. Katie was walking slightly in front of us, then she froze in front of the double doors of the large sitting room that lay open.

A little hand clutched mine. Amandine turned to me. She whispered, "I don't like it in that room either: the bad picture is in there."

"What bad picture?" I asked.

Amandine spoke English but she also spoke the French of her mother. I told her to call me Erica and that my friend was called Katie. She said once more, "My name is Amandine, but Daddy calls me Mandy."

My heart skipped a beat. I was stunned and lost for words when she then said, "I call her Mummy, but Daddy calls Mummy, Elise. Daddy is not here anymore. He called me Mandy and I liked that, but Daddy isn't here anymore, he has gone to Heaven."

There was a tear running down her face.

She started to cry.

My heart stopped a beat. I had found my sister's child and discovered that Elise Du Sante survived the train crash. My heart was fluttering so much so that I almost fainted, when suddenly with his arm around her waist, James helped the worn-out Elise Du Sante to walk with her daughter to the other side of the chateau.

"Maman, Maman," Amandine cried.

Elise, her face gaunt, tried to speak but she couldn't. She simply said, "Help us, please."

Otto lifted Elise as though she were no more than a doll. Katie took Amandine's hand, and together we went through the chateau and down the stairs.

"You have to leave now," Otto said. "There is a car outside with the engine running. You leave now with James. I can't go with you, but you are in safe hands with him. Don't stop and don't ask questions. Just go. There is a big storm brewing."

No sooner had they run to the car than thunder roared and there was a flash of lightening. Rain was now pounding against the door. Otto said, "Gather everyone up. We must leave here now. Leave everything behind."

There was no comment from us – we just ran as fast as we could through the battering rain with James helping Elise, and me half carrying Amandine.

Outside, a large limousine was idling. Henri was in the driver's seat with James sitting beside him. I sighed with relief as Amandine, Elise and I got into the car before Katie climbed in after us.

Henri started the engine, and the car began to crawl. "Hey, wait a minute we're moving, where's Otto?" Katie cried out.

"He will not be coming with us," Henri said. "Just get in the car, Katie."

"What?" Katie said as she reached for the door handle. Henri turned around quickly and, just as though he was speaking to a child, Henri said, "Katie, my dear, James has told you before, and I have told you a hundred times." He was angry "Perhaps my English is not good enough for you, Katie, but if you attempt to open that door, I will stop and put you out, then drive away, leaving you to walk alone back to Paris. It is a cold, wet dark night and that would take you two or maybe three days to reach Paris, if you survive that is. Furthermore, when alone, you do not know what might await you out there. If it was not so serious, Katie, I would stop and leave you to walk alone right now, because a few steps into the dark and you would be back."

Katie was angry. "Stop speaking to me as if I was a child. I don't get this. I am sure if I ask Otto, he would take us all back to Paris."

I said, "He would certainly take you somewhere." Still frustrated, I snapped at her, "Katie, this is not a fairy story."

"No, it's not. Erica, talk sense to her," Henri said, almost pleading. "I am afraid things may turn out badly for you, Katie," he said. "By now you must know that Otto is here to protect us. I know you are very fond of him, but Otto is not here just for you, Katie. Otto has been sent here by a higher being to destroy the demon hiding in the shadows of Chateau Langedechu. Inside a painting."

"What! Are you joking? In a painting?" Katie asked. "Which painting is it? Is it the winged angel?"

"No, Katie," he said, "the figure in the painting that you have seen is portrayed as a handsome young man with beautiful white wings. Katie, look closely at the painting and you will see, it is a malevolent supernatural being. His face is distorted and intimidating, his ears are pointed, and his piercing eyes glow red with malice. If you look even further, you will see there are horns protruding from its head. It is a portrait of a demon, Katie. If you do not stop, I will turn this car around and leave you there for the demon to find you. Now do you understand?"

Henri looked round at Katie's forlorn face. "Come Katie, I saw you study the portrait. He is muscular and handsome and powerful, and yet you must sense his malevolence.

"The Langedechu, Katie. He is the Fallen Angel. I saw you admire the painting on the wall. It is a painting of Lucifer portrayed as a handsome young man. He is one of the fallen angels who haunt this chateau. Do you now understand why we cannot go back there. Only Otto would dare to return because Otto is a high-ranking angel."

Katie gasped with shock. Henri said, "Yes, Katie. He is one of a hierarchy of God's angels, and he will be here again. For a short time, he will be part of your world.

"We all must leave now, with the exception of Otto, who will destroy the creature before he leaves. The chateau too will be destroyed, and we must never, ever go near that chateau or the land it lies on again."

And so, we left the chateau grounds, James, Henri, Katie, Elise, Amandine, and me. No sooner had the limousine's door closed than I looked back at the heavy mist that was gathering again around the chateau. The mist had become so dense that the chateau disappeared into it.

"Wait a minute. Are we waiting here until the fog disappears?" Katie asked. I mean, is it going to be a long time? Because you know the markets close early."

Henri sighed, "We are all leaving now, Katie."

"Oh, thank goodness," Katie said. "Henri, you being such an obliging person. Do you think on the way back from here you could drop me off at the market. You see, there is a shop on the way back there that has a beautiful green silk dress, and I know it would fit me, but Erica, whom you know can be quite selfish sometimes, would never let me stop there."

"Good," Henri said, "I am glad someone has sense."

I said, "OK, go get it, Katie. I will not stop you this time. I will even buy it, and you can wear that green dress."

"Really? You would buy it? That's very generous of you, Erica, but I couldn't let you buy it. I am sure you would like to have it yourself, Erica, because it looks so expensive, and you always buy expensive clothes…"

Erica said, "I promise, if it's still there, Katie, I will buy it for you…"

"What! Why?" Katie asked. "Why the sudden bout of generosity? You wouldn't even stop to let me look at it this morning. So, what changed your mind?"

"I will want you to wear it as a Matron of Honour that's all."

"A Matron of Honour! A what!?" Katie almost choked. "Did I hear you right?"

"Yes, and before you ask, I did have an offer of marriage today, from James.

Katie was stunned. "Today? Well, that is a surprise," she said.

I sighed, "Yes, Katie, he proposed, and I accepted his proposal."

Katie cried out, "Oh, my God! What a relief. Did you not see my heart stop for a moment. I thought it was Otto you were going to marry."

"Well, that has been a long-time coming, Erica, and I am so glad it is James who proposed."

"Tell her, Erica," James said, almost whispering.

"I heard that, tell her what?" Katie asked. "You should have married Erica long ago, Mr Smart Alec. You better marry her now because I was so looking forward to this wedding, and that dress!" she said with a loud sigh. "It will be your fault if I don't get that dress."

I said, "Katie, get in the car with Elise and Amandine please, or there won't be a wedding. Don't ask me to explain anymore, just go. You need to go now."

Sighing, Katie got in the car and rolled down the window. She had one more try. "But what about Otto? I can travel with him. That would suit me better."

"I am sure it would, but no, Katie. Otto is staying here with James and me."

Annoyed, Katie said, "Look, it's OK. Don't panic. I can cope, and you are doing it again. I know now what Otto is. He told me everything and now you don't have to watch me. I will be alright with him."

James said, "You will not be with him, Katie, because he will be here with me, and you will be out buying that green dress, the one you love so much." James was always gentle when he spoke to Katie, much in the way one might speak to a disappointed child. He said, "Now, Katie, do I have to physically put you in the car?"

Katie folded her arms. "Just try it," she said. "I am staying."

To Katie's surprise, James swept her off her feet, carried her across the drive and dropped her like a sack of coal in the back seat of the car. She was livid. James tried to be nice. He said, "Go with Elise and Amadine, Katie, and get your green dress. We have to close the chateau now. Otto and I have to find and destroy the thing that is lurking in the mist."

I tripped, almost knocking James over, and fell back, panicking. Katie was upset but her childlike behaviour changed when Erica said, "Katie, I know you know and understand the power of the wormholes. We must close the one at Langedechu before the Crone gets her hands on it."

Otto said, "The key lies within the painting you have seen of the winged demon. We have to get that key before the Crone does. Then we will lock it up forever."

Like a spoiled child, Katie smiled and got into the car and it pulled away quickly. We stood there waving to Amandine as the limousine-taxi took off. Then James and I went with Otto back into the chateau. I was terrified.

I was physically shaking. I took James's hand as we followed Otto and climbed the stairs before us and stopped at the door.

As he turned the handle on the door, Otto said to me, "Do not be afraid. Though you cannot see them, we have a cohort of angels, ghostly and on guard duty. The black-winged figure you will see again in the painting is of the demon sent by the Crone. The painting is no ordinary work of art.

"In the painting behind the portrayal of a door is an entrance. Otto reached and moved the painting a little. I panicked as I was sure I saw the creature in the painting move. To my horror, Otto said, "Yes, it lives. It seeks the key to the wormhole here. It knows that it is within the painting itself."

I looked up at the painting of the black winged creature and I felt sick. I had butterflies in my stomach. As I looked closely, I could swear it moved; this creature was alive in the canvas. How could that be? To my horror, it turned and looked at me with its red slits for eyes and a tongue hanging from its mouth with drips that were of dark blood.

Stupidly, I tried thinking it was just my imagination. I reached out and touched the painting and Otto screamed at me, "No, no, do not touch anything, not yet." But I had already touched the canvas with a finger and, to my horror, some blood dripped onto my hand and, what was worse, it was warm and thickening. In a moment, there in my hand was a key, completely covered in this thick blood.

Otto squeezed my other hand. He said, "Look closely. The painting and the wormhole within it there will be an opening."

I was so afraid; nothing in this world could explain why there was movement in the painting. I could see a gap like an entrance to a tunnel. It was opening and closing, as though the whole of the painting was alive. It was moving undulating like waves in a calm sea. I was sure I could hear breathing. Then I could hear something calling my name from within the painting. It froze me; I couldn't move. Then Otto was calling my name over and over. He came to me and shook me like a rag doll "Erica, Erica, you must now put your hand into the painting."

"No," I was horrified. "I can't do that!" I turned away and I tried to leave, "Please Otto, help me." I was shaking like a leaf. He put his hand on my shoulder and immediately I felt calm.

A haze came over me and I saw the painting appeared to have come to life. The hole in the centre of the painting began to widen every second, undulating in and out as it as if it were alive. Worse still, I could hear a breathing sound from the canvas that grew louder with each passing moment.

I was shivering, terrified, and I tried to leave but my feet had turned to lead, and I couldn't move. Otto caught my arm. "Wait," he said, "Wait and watch. It's over now – they are here."

I grabbed Otto's arm. "Who's here?" I asked. "Who are you talking about? Otto the whole canvas is now moving, how can that be?"

More clouds were forming in the painting. They were so thick that they looked like dark grey cotton wool. It was a thick mist that seemed to be taking the shape of emaciated human beings. I couldn't move. I was terrified of what was in front of me. It was more creatures like the ones in the paintings in the chateau, only they looked alive. Though it looked like a painting, it was moving and the deep black, foul-smelling creatures had human shaped bodies covered in scales, but only the largest of the monsters had a tail that whipped back and forth like a whip.

As though unable to move, the creature stood like a statue staring at us. I almost fainted when I saw it was moving, coming slowly towards us. I held my breath. I couldn't move. "James!" I cried, "I can't move!" He didn't answer; he was staring at the black beast as though he too was hypnotised. I called to Otto.

"Otto, please answer me," I cried. I wanted to run to him, but suddenly I couldn't move either. I couldn't move my arms James too stood frozen like a statue.

Otto said, "Listen, there is a voice coming from the painting!"

"Those who sin and are about to die must bow to the dark angel."

"Erica, do not bow to this creature," Otto said as he grabbed my arm and pulled me away from the painting. "We must get James and be away from here before dusk. If we do not make it but reach only the edge of the wormhole, we could be sucked in to face the fires of Hell."

I looked and saw Otto had blood on his hands. He had taken the key. I felt movement at my back.

Otto cried, "Erica, you and you alone must now throw the key into the hole. Only you can close the wormhole!" He handed me the warm metal key, still covered with the black things and blood.

Otto cried out, "Now Erica, throw it now! Throw it into the hole before she can reach you. She is powerful. She wants the key to the wormhole that lies here in your hands. Now Erica, throw it and close that wormhole forever!"

I knew her the moment I laid eyes on her. I knew it was the Crone. I did what Otto asked and there was the most terrifying and blood curdling scream I had ever heard, and now I could see her, the woman in the painting. The huge painting had come alive; there on the canvas was the old woman who was screaming in anger. She floated into the painting only to be frozen and unable to move. She was trapped. The moment I heard her, I knew it was the Crone – the demon from hell.

Otto said, "This is the closest we will get to escape. We all must run now, less we be trapped in that painting and sucked into the wormhole. The painting must be destroyed."

No sooner had he said that than I saw James hold up and throw what looked like a large, beautiful gold crucifix into the hole. Then there was laughter and screaming that made my blood run cold. She was there. I could see her floating closer. It was the Crone.

"The Crone is here for the key. Throw it in, Erica!" Otto said, "Now, you must do it and the gate will close."

I threw it into the hole. It was whirling and a scream came from it that almost burst my eardrums. My hands over my ears were dripping blood from the key and I passed out.

I don't know how long I was unconscious but when I woke up, I was in Henri's car, travelling to Paris. I sat in the front, with James.

James said, "It's all over, Erica. Thanks to Otto, you have closed that wormhole." James tried to cheer me. "That's two down, Erica, and two to go. Though, for all we know and pray, with the help of the angels, the remaining wormholes will be closed. They are somewhere in the world, and you will be free of any creature that would aim to contact you or harm you ever again. You are safe now, as I promised. The Crone has been sent back to Hell and kept there by a cohort of Angels that have been sent to Otto from Heaven to protect all of you – Henri, Katie, Elise and Amandine. You are all safe and always will be."

To this day, I don't know what happened. There had been an almighty bang, and I passed out. Incredible as it seems, it had been two years until I woke up in a hospital bed. I woke up to see some men in white coats and nurses in uniform. I heard them say, "She is going to be fine." To me they added, "There are good friends of yours here. They have been waiting for almost two years to see you smile again."

I didn't know where I was until someone put their arms around me. I didn't recognise her at first and then I thanked God it was Katie. Then all the familiar faces were coming closer. It transpired I had been in a coma for two years.

After Katie had almost hugged me to death, I saw James sitting on a chair beside my bed. He took my hand and kissed it. He was smiling, and I saw tears in his eyes.

He said, "That's some sleep you have had, Madam. You have kept me waiting." He added, "You woke up in nice time. Henri has arranged the wedding ceremony for us."

Katie said, "James bought me the green dress. I can't wait to wear it. The doctors have given you the news you can go home. Henri has chartered a plane, and we are all taking you home to Lanshoud today."

I cried tears of happiness.

www.ingramcontent.com/pod-product-compliance
Lightning Source LLC
Chambersburg PA
CBHW050822180626
46814CB00004B/1413